The Littlest Hitler

The Littlest Hitler

Stories

Ryan Boudinot

COUNTERPOINT
A Member of the Perseus Books Group
New York

Copyright © 2006 by Ryan Boudinot
Published by Counterpoint,
A Member of the Perseus Books Group

"The Littlest Hitler" appeared in *The Mississippi Review, The Best American
    Nonrequired Reading 2003*, and *Il Diario* (Italy) (2002–2003).
"On Sex and Relationships" appeared on Nerve.com (2006).
"Bee Beard" appeared in *Los Angeles Review* (2006).
"My Mother Was a Monster" appeared in *BlackBook* (2004) and *The Revolution
    Will Be Accessorized:* BlackBook *Presents Dispatches from the New
    Counterculture* (2006).
"Profession" appeared in *Hobart* (2003).
"Civilization" appeared in *McSweeney's* (2004).
"Written by Machines" appeared in *Bullfight Review* (2004).
"Absolut Boudinot" appeared on Eyeshot.net (2004).
"Newholly" appeared in *Stumbling and Raging: More Politically Inspired Fiction* (2005).

Counterpoint books are available at special discounts for bulk purchases in the
United States by corporations, institutions, and other organizations. For more
information, please contact the Special Markets Department at the Perseus Books
Group, 11 Cambridge Center, Cambridge MA 02142, or call (617) 252-5298 or
(800) 255-1514, or e-mail special.markets@perseusbooks.com.

Designed by Brent Wilcox

Library of Congress Cataloging-in-Publication Data
Boudinot, Ryan, 1972-
    The littlest Hitler : stories / Ryan Boudinot.
        p.   cm.
    ISBN-13: 978-1-58243-357-8 (hardcover : alk. paper)
    ISBN-10: 1-58243-357-7 (hardcover : alk. paper)
    I. Title.
    PS3602.O888L57   2006
    813'.6—dc22

                                                                            2006006260

06 07 08 / 10 9 8 7 6 5 4 3 2 1

For Jen and Miles

Contents

The Littlest
Hitler

Then there's the time I went as Hitler for Halloween.
I had gotten the idea after watching World War II week on PBS,
but my dad helped me make the costume. I wore tan polyester
pants and one of my dad's khaki shirts, with sleeves so long they
dragged on the floor unless I rolled them up. With some paints
left over from when we made the pinewood derby car for YMCA
Indian Guides, he painted a black swastika in a white circle on a
red bandanna and tied it around my left arm. Using the Dippity-
Doo he put in his hair every morning, he gave my own hair that
plastered, parted style that had made Hitler look like he was always sweating. We clipped the sides off a fifty-cent mustache and
adhered it to my upper lip with liquid latex. I tucked my pants
into the black rubber boots I had to wear whenever I played outside and stood in front of the mirror. My dad laughed and said,
"I guarantee it, Davy. You're going to be the scariest kid in fourth
grade."

My school had discouraged trick-or-treating since the razor
blade and thumbtack incidents of 1982. Instead, they held a

Harvest Carnival, not officially called "Halloween" so as not to upset the churchy types. Everyone at school knew the carnival was for wimps. All week before Halloween the kids had been separating themselves into two camps, those who got to go trick-or-treating, and those who didn't. My dad was going to take me to the carnival, since I, like everybody else, secretly wanted to go. Then we'd go trick-or-treating afterward.

There were problems with my costume as soon as I got on the bus that morning. "Heil Hitlah!" a couple of big kids in the back chanted until Mrs. Reese pulled over to reprimand them. We knew it was serious when she pulled over, being that the last pulling-over incident occurred when Carl Worthington cut off one of Ginger Lopez's pigtails with a pair of scissors stolen from the library.

"That isn't polite language appropriate for riding the bus!" Mrs. Reese said. "Do you talk like that around the dinner table? I want you both in the front seats and as soon as we get to school I'm marching you to Mr Warnekc's office."

"But I didn't do anything!"

I felt somewhat vindicated but guilty at the same time for causing this ruckus. Everybody was looking at me with these grim expressions. It's important, I suppose, to note that there wasn't a single Jewish person on the bus. Or in our school, for that matter. In fact, there was only one Jewish family in our town, the Friedlanders, and their kids didn't go to West Century Elementary because they were home-schooled freaks.

When I got to school Mrs. Thompson considered me for a moment in the doorway and seemed torn, both amused and disturbed at the implications of a fourth-grade Hitler. When she called roll I stood up sharply from my desk, did the *Sieg Heil* salute I'd been practicing in front of the TV, and shouted, "Here!" Some people laughed.

After roll was taken we took out our spelling books, but Mrs. Thompson had other ideas. "Some of you might have noticed we have a historical figure in our class today. While the rest of you dressed up as goblins and fairies and witches, it looks like Davy is the only one who chose to come as a real-life person."

"I'm a real-life person, too, Mrs. Thompson."

"And who would you be, Lisette?"

"I'm Anne Frank."

Mrs. Thompson put a hand to her lips. Clearly she didn't know how to handle this. I'd never paid much attention to Lisette before. She'd always been one of the smart, pretty girls who everyone likes. When I saw her rise from her desk with a lopsided Star of David made of yellow construction paper pinned to her Austrian-looking frock or whatever you call it, I felt the heat of her nine-year-old loathing pounding me in the face.

"This is quite interesting," Mrs. Thompson said, "being that you both came as figures from World War II. Maybe you can educate us about what you did. Davy, if you could tell us what you know about Hitler."

I cleared my throat. "He was a really, really mean guy."

"What made him so mean?"

"Well, he made a war and killed a bunch of people and made everybody think like him. He only ate vegetables and his wife was his niece. He kept his blood in jars. Somebody tried to kill him with a suitcase and then he took some poison and died."

"What people did he kill?"

"Everybody. He didn't like Jesse Owens because he was Afro-American."

"Yes, but mostly what kind of people did he have problems with?"

"He killed all the Jews."

"Not all Jews, fortunately, but millions of them. Including Anne Frank."

The classroom was riveted. I didn't know whether I was in trouble or what. Lisette smirked at me when Mrs. Thompson said her character's name, then walked to the front of the class to tell us about her.

"Anne Frank lived in Holland during World War II. And when the Nazis invaded she lived in someone's attic with her family and some other people. She wrote in her diary every day and liked movie stars. She wanted to grow up to write stories for a newspaper, but the Nazis got her and her family and made them go to a concentration camp and killed them. A concentration camp is a place where they burn people in ovens. Then somebody found her diary and everybody liked it."

When Lisette was done everybody clapped. George Ford, who sat in front of me and was dressed as Mr. T, turned around, lowered his eyes, and shook his fist at me. "I pity the foo who kills all the Jews."

Recess was a nightmare.

I was followed around the playground by Lisette's friends, who were playing horse with a jump rope, berating me for Anne Frank's death.

"How would you like it if you had to live in an attic and pee in a bucket and couldn't walk around or talk all day and didn't have much food to eat?"

It didn't take long for them to make me cry. The rule about recess was you couldn't go back into the building until the bell, so I had to wait before I could get out of my costume. I got knots in my stomach thinking about the parade at the end of the day. Everybody else seemed so happy in their costumes. And then Lisette started passing around a piece of notebook paper that said "We're on Anne Frank's Side" and all these people signed it. When my friend Charlie got the paper he tore it up and said to the girls, "Leave Davy alone! He just wanted to be a scary bad guy for Halloween and he *didn't really kill anybody!*"

"I should just go as someone else," I said, sitting beneath the slide while some kids pelted it with pea gravel. This was Charlie's and my fort for when we played GI Joe.

"They can kiss my grits," Charlie said. He was dressed as a deadly galactic robot with silver spray-painted cardboard tubes for arms and a pair of new-wave sunglasses. "This is a free country, ain't it? Hey! Stop throwing those son-of-a-bitching rocks!"

"Charlie!"

"Oops. Playground monitor. Time for warp speed." Charlie pulled on his thumb, made a clicking sound, and disappeared under the tire tunnel.

Despite Charlie's moral support, I peeled my mustache off and untied my armband as soon as I made it to the boys' room. There were three fifth-graders crammed into a stall, going, "Oh, *man*! There's *corn* in it!" None of them seemed to notice me whimpering by the sink.

Mrs. Thompson gave me her gray-haired wig to wear for the parade.

"Here, Davy. You can be an old man. An old man who likes to wear khaki."

I knew Mrs. Thompson was trying to humor me and I resented her for it. Lisette, for whatever reason, maybe because her popularity in our classroom bordered on totalitarian, got to lead the parade. I was stuck between Becky Lewis and her pathetic cat outfit and Doug Becker, dressed as a garden. His mom and dad were artists. Each carrot, radish, and potato had been crafted in meticulous papier mache, painted, lacquered, and halfway embedded in a wooden platform he wore around his waist. The platform represented a cross section, with brown corduroys painted with rocks and earthworms symbolizing dirt, and his fake leaf-covered shirt playing the part of a trellis. For the third year in a row Doug ended up winning the costume contest.

By the time our parade made it to the middle school I was thoroughly demoralized. I had grown so weary of being asked,

"What *are* you?" that I had taken to wearing the wig over my face and angrily answering, "I'm *lint*! I'm *lint*!"

My dad made wood stoves for a living. When my mom left he converted our living room into a shop, which was embarrassing when my friends came over because the inside of our house was always at least ninety degrees. My dad was genuinely disappointed when he learned of my classmates' reactions.

"But everyone knows you're not prejudiced. It's Halloween for crying out loud." He folded the bandanna, looking sad and guilty. "I'm sorry, Davy. We didn't mean for it to turn out like this, did we? Tell you what. Let's go to Sprouse-Reitz and buy you the best goddamn costume they got."

We drove into town in the blue pickup we called Fleetwood Mack. Smooth like a Cadillac, built like a Mack truck. The Halloween aisle at 6:30 P.M. on October 31st is pretty slim pickings. There was a little girl with her mom fussing over a ballerina outfit—last-minute shoppers like us. I basically had a choice between a pig mask, some cruddy do-it-yourself face paint deals, and a discounted Frankenstein mask with a torn jaw.

"Hey! Lookit! Frankenstein!" my dad said, trying to invest some enthusiasm in the ordeal. "Don't worry about the jaw, we'll just duct tape it from the inside. Nobody'll even notice."

"I want a mask with real hair. Not fake plastic lumpy hair," I said.

"You don't really have a choice here, Davy. Unless you want the pig mask."

"Fine. I'll go as stupid Frankenstein."

My dad grabbed me by the elbow and spun me around. "Do you want a Halloween this year or not? You can't go tricker treating without a costume and this is about your only option. Otherwise it's just you and me sitting on our asses in front of the television tonight."

That night the grade school gym floor was covered with the same smelly red tarp they used every year for the PTA Ham Dinner. Teachers and high school students worked in booths like the Ring Toss, Goin' Fishin', and the Haunted Maze, a complex of cardboard duct-taped together. All the parents were nervously eyeing Cyndy Dartmouth, who'd come as a hooker. She was the same seventh grader who'd shocked everybody by actually dyeing her hair blonde for her famous person report on Marilyn Monroe. Her parents ran the baseball card shop in town and every middle school guy in West Century wanted to get into her pants. She seemed womanly and incredibly sophisticated to me as we stood in line together for the maze. I liked her because she stuck up for me on the bus and one time told me what a tampon was.

They let you into the maze two at a time, and Cyndy and I ended up going in together.

"You go first," I said as we entered the gaping cardboard dragon's mouth. She got on her hands and knees in front of me and for an incredible moment I saw her panties under her black leather skirt.

The maze took a sharp right turn and the light disappeared. Cyndy reached back and grabbed my arm. I screamed. She laughed and I tried to pretend I wasn't scared. The eighth graders had done a really good job building this place. There were glow-in-the-dark eyes on both walls and a speaker up ahead playing a spooky sound effects album. I held onto her fishnet ankle and begged her to let us go back. We passed a sign reading "Watch Out for Bears!!!" and entered a tunnel covered in fake fur. I started crying. Cyndy held me, whispering it was all just made up, none of it was real, it was just cardboard stuck together with tape, holding my face in that magical place between her breasts that smelled like perfume from the mall.

Suddenly light streamed in on us. One of the high school volunteers had heard me crying and opened a panel in the ceiling.

"Ross! Mike! Check it out! They're totally doing it in here!" the guy laughed. I looked up to see four heads crowding around the opening.

"Leave us alone, you fuckers!" Cyndy said, and it seemed a miraculous act of generosity that she didn't tell them the real reason for our embrace.

We quickly crawled through the rest of the maze. When we emerged a group of kids was waiting for us.

"Hey Cyndy, why don't you crawl through the tunnel with a guy who's actually got pubes?"

I panicked, hoping my dad wouldn't hear. I didn't want Cyndy to get picked on, but I kind of liked the idea that the other kids thought I'd done something naughty with her in the maze. When Ross Roberts asked me if I'd gotten any, I sort of shrugged, as if to suggest that I had, although I didn't completely understand what it was I could have gotten.

Cyndy bit her bottom lip and disappeared into the girls' room with three other girls who would end up sending me hate notes on her behalf the next day at school. The rest of the carnival was awful after that. I carried my Frankenstein mask upside down because I'd forgotten to bring a candy bag. Most of the candy at the carnival was that sugarless diabetic crap, handed out simply because one kid in sixth grade had diabetes and we all had to be fair to him. My dad walked around the perimeter of the gym, pretending to be interested in each grade's autumn crafts project, not really mingling with any of the other adults, even though he'd sold wood stoves to a few of them. I could tell he didn't want to be here and when I told him I wanted to leave he nodded and said it was time to do some serious trick-or-treating.

I liked my dad because he didn't seem to follow a lot of the rules other grown-ups seemed obligated to follow. He let me watch R-rated movies, showed me how to roll joints, and told me how to sneak into movie theaters. We bought our Fourth of July fireworks from the Indian reservation and used them to blow up slugs. The only times I felt like he was a real grown-up were when he was figuring out the bills or being sad about my mom. But tonight we were the closest of co-conspirators. In Fleetwood Mack we sang along to the Steve Miller *Greatest Hits* tape and picked the richest-looking neighborhoods to trick-or-treat in.

With a greasy Burger King bag salvaged from the floor of the truck, we went door-to-door, my dad hanging out behind me, waving politely. Somebody even tossed him a can of beer.

I didn't know we were at the Friedlanders' house until Mrs. Friedlander opened the door. Word had it they were among the parents who didn't let their kids go trick-or-treating since the razor blade and thumbtack scare of 1982. Hannah Friedlander sat on the steps up to the second story of their split-level house, leaning over in her sorceress costume to see who it was. Mike, her brother, came up the stairs from the rec room and joined her, breathing dramatically in his Darth Vader mask. I wanted to do something nice for them, wanted to just hand them my whole bag, but I couldn't bring myself to do it. I'd be too embarrassed, I'd make my father angry, I'd call too much attention to the fact they couldn't go trick-or-treating. So I chose to do nothing but accept Mrs. Friedlander's individually-wrapped Swiss chocolate balls and thanked her, then walked back to Fleetwood Mack with my dad and drove home, looking at all the Halloween displays through the nostrils of Frankenstein's nose.

"So did you have an okay Halloween after all?" my dad asked, carrying me upstairs to my bedroom. I nodded and got into my pjs, then pulled the covers over my face and let him bite my nose through the blanket like he did every night. Later, when I could hear him snoring through the wall, I took the bag of candy from my dresser and tiptoed downstairs to what used to be our living room. There was a stove hooked up to each of our three chimneys, one which was cold, one with some embers inside, the third filled with flames. I opened the door to the flaming stove and thought about throwing my whole bag in there, but then remembered the rule: wood and paper only. Besides, I had an entire Snickers bar in there; I wasn't insane. I sat for a long time, eating chocolates one by one in front of the fire, then plunged my hand into the stove to see how far it could go before it really started to hurt.

On Sex and
Relationships

We hadn't seen Bob and Julianne since their wedding, so when our schedules meshed we pulled a couple premillennial bottles of Screaming Eagle from our cellar and drove to their house in the part of town near the lifestyle center with the Apple store, Crate and Barrel, and Anthropologie. Katherine and I met B&J when the female halves of us were in grad school. The women could argue about Slavoj Žižek while Bob and I scrolled through the lists of interests we had in common, like vintage amps and data mining. It worked, the four of us. We'd leave each others' apartments feeling satiated with cheer, tell our partners on the ride home how much we enjoyed hanging with the other couple, include each other on funny email threads. Katherine endured bridesmaid hell for their wedding; Bob and I jammed a few times in a storage shed near the freeway. Bob's and my creative powers had waned, siphoned into these things we got paid to do. Bob was going prematurely bald and I was prematurely gray. I urged Bob to shave his head and reformat it with a goatee;

he convinced me to return to my punk roots and go for bright orange hair, which lent me some fleeting cred with my underlings at the technology company but provoked a bitter argument with Katherine, who said I needed to get serious about something, and no, just because I'd recently hit six figures in the salary department didn't mean I was de facto serious. That's about the time the wedding went down and Julianne returned for a third helping of education to get certified as a Montessori teacher while Bob, basically retirable at 32 thanks to stock options, cycled through a series of consulting gigs for wireless companies. I invented an application that made it easier to create cell phone ring tones. Hilariously, we found ourselves more successful than anyone we had ever known personally. We were human benchmarks. And for whatever reason, schedules, fatigue maybe, Katherine and I left the orbit of our friends for months until I got this email from Julianne saying, Dude what's up, and, Hey we just bought this kickin' new barbecue. Come on over and enjoy some Indian food. Bring your bad selves.

To visit old friends, this is what I'm talking about. To walk into their house and see the books they read as undergrads lining the bookcases as you pet their dog. To hand them a deliberately dusty bottle of wine while the women's voices ring off each other at a higher register than usual. I love these friendships, squeezing my chest against my best friend's wife's breasts, feeling her bra strap as I press my hand to her back.

"B&J," I said.

"Guys!" Julianne said.

B&J had renovated their place, laying down eco-friendly bamboo hardwood and crown molding, replacing the plastic light switch plates with ones made of chrome, getting all Restoration Hardware on the mantle, sconces, and heat registers. Kind of put Katherine and me to shame. We still had a room full of U-Haul boxes slated to become a place to do yoga in. But B&J, man, they looked good. Julianne had clearly been working the hell out of her upper body. Bob had bought a new pair of glasses that made him look like Harry Potter or an architect. Whatever was cooking on the grill outside smelled really fantastic. Turns out theirs wasn't your typical suburban barbecue but an actual Indian tandoor. They'd bought it from a developer who dumped it on craigslist for cheap before he returned to Bangalore. Pretty sweet. We drank beer from pilsner glasses chilled in the freezer and helped Bob make the naan. This was a summer night, short-sleeves-in-the-dark kind of weather. Work came up as a subject of discussion, and Bob and I sorted through geeked-out anecdotes, speaking of rounds of financing, platforms, system migration. We still referred to our employers as "they" because only drink-the-Koolaid drones referred to their employers as "we." We'd erected fortifications around the parts of our personalities that remained intact after perversely houred work weeks. That's why we were here, in chaise lounges on their new deck still smelling of sealant, pretending we didn't give a shit about portfolios or due diligence. This was the part of the conversation about stuff they'd done to the house, with Bob waving his hand and talking about a dishwasher he'd completely fucked up. We talked about this stuff before we got to the sentences that started with the word *remember*. That happened after the naan and during the three distinct curries Julianne unleashed upon us, washed down with some of our wine, which didn't really match the curries at all, but was excusable after a couple microbrews.

Remember that camping trip where we took mushrooms and went out in the canoe at four in the morning to watch the sunrise from the middle of the lake?

Remember that fucked up roommate of yours who listened to Joy Division thirty hours straight and always denied that he drank our orange juice?

These became less like questions and more like remonstrations. Remember! . . . when the car broke down. Remember! . . . when you lost that earring and we had to go back across the Canadian border to retrieve it. Remember! . . . when you thought you had testicular cancer. Into my second glass of wine, my mouth a riot of flaming spice and laughter, I faced down the truth that soon we'd think of these friends of ours as people to add to the Christmas card list. I thought of myself racing toward the stinking corpse I was destined to become. It made me want to puke into their new pedestal sink. I accepted another glass.

Then there's that part where the guys go do one thing while the women do another, and in this case it meant me going down to the basement to check out the Marshall half stack Bob'd been rebuilding. The monster had been trashed and decimated for parts when he bought the cabinet and head. Bob explained how he'd purchased a rare kind of British tubes off eBay, soldered the amp back to life, nurtured it to a scrotum-tightening crunch.

Bob handed me his cherry red Gibson SG and plugged me in. "Go ahead," he said, "gimme a good power chord." I hit a muffled G and goddamn if it didn't feel really nice. The amp was cranked loud enough to move my pant legs thanks to air displacement. I knew the women upstairs were sharing a sweetly denigrating comment about us. I played some bars of songs I knew parts of, "Smells Like Teen Spirit," "Black Dog," "Walk This Way." Never the whole songs, just parts. Which made it notable when Bob plugged in his Gibson hollow body and said, "I've been working on this project for six months. Some guys make a goal to scale Everest. Me, well, just check this out." Upon which he proceeded to play "Stairway to Heaven" note for *fucking* note. And sing at the same time. Even Jimmy Page didn't do that. And by note for note, I mean he didn't fake his way through the solos. Every lick was in there as far as I could tell. His singing was shit, of course, but he'd learned the whole song and played it through to the end. Around *then the piper will lead us to reason,* the women descended and sat on the basement steps and smiled, bobbing their heads, imitating stoners from the seventies they were too young to have actually been. When Bob finished, we all clapped and I said, "Wow, man, that is some accomplishment." Bob shrugged, put his guitar back in the case and set it next to an aborted experiment about growing some pot with heat lamps.

"Tell him about the website," Julianne said.

"It's kind of stupid. I started this site for guys like me who want to learn 'Stairway,'" Bob said.

"What are you talking about, it's got almost a thousand registered users," Julianne said.

"Yeah, I kind of got carried away with it. There are tutorials and tablature and a board."

"Oh yeah, what's the URL?" Katherine said.

"Ooohitmakesmewonder.com," Bob said.

As I cracked up I couldn't help register surprise that Bob hadn't told me about the site. I stopped myself. What the hell had happened? Me with hurt feelings that a guy I used to do knife tokes with in adult student housing hadn't asked me to learn "Stairway to Heaven" with him? I was primarily a bassist anyway.

Back upstairs someone said, "Why don't we hang in the living room?" Julianne sat with her bare feet tucked beneath her, swirling another glass of wine, and here, with an iPod shuffling through a playlist titled "Mellow," we talked incredulously and uninformedly of politics until Julianne and Bob looked at each other and Katherine and I knew something was about to get told to us.

"We're trying to have a baby," Julianne said. Smiles and more high-pitched voices from the women. My knee-jerk imagination had my friends fucking. There was Bob rubbing his dick against that tattoo on the small of Julianne's back. There were Julianne's legs, up around Bob's shoulders, giving him some of that *Kama Sutra* action. Then they were talking about how incredibly *difficult* it is to get pregnant, how we're brainwashed through sex ed into thinking the condom or pill is the only thing keeping you from childrearing oblivion. "It's more like tossing a dart at a dartboard," Julianne said. "Everyone can hit a bull's-eye but it usually takes a while." Katherine then broached the subject of childbirth styles, and true to our nonconformist roots we all agreed midwives and birth centers were the way to go, with all the candles and harp music that went along with it. I knew that on the drive home later that night every word out of Katherine's mouth would glom onto this single subject, having kids, and why it was such a horrible idea.

I followed Bob back into the kitchen for more wine. "Man it's crazy," he said, "the idea of me being a dad. Seems like a giant time suck. We're trying to see as many movies as we can right now, go on some burly hiking trips. Because when Julianne gets pregnant, I just know we're going to be homebodies."

"Totally," I said, which was all I felt like saying. He wanted me to egg him on, give him a chance to riff on the rites of paternity, but instead I got him talking about how he figured out the really hard solo at the end.

When we returned to the living room Julianne was showing Katherine a kit of some sort, a little box that included a thermometer. Julianne said, "I've been checking my temp every hour or so; obsessed, I know." Shrugging, she stuck it in her mouth, putting the impetus on Bob to converse.

"What about you guys," Bob said. "Thinking about kids?"

Kind of a direct question, and yet it did seem to draw a line under the fact we had lost touch with each other. It was the kind of question you ask people you don't know very well. The understanding now was that Katherine and I were expected to proclaim our procreative intentions. Our friends really should have been more tip-toey about it, knowing about Katherine's abortion two years before. That had been a fucked up time. Katherine and I split, came back together, slept with some other people, repeated the cycle a couple more times until, exhausted, we clung to the remnants of each other and realized no one else would have ever put up with this much shit. Thankfully B&J had been there with some no-bullshit conversation and therapeutic Thai food to help us get through it. At one point I literally vomited in a gutter, if memory serves. Julianne had told me that my and Katherine's love was like that between John Cassavetes and Gena Rowlands, tempestuous but unstoppable. I remember nodding like I knew who those people were.

"We're thinking about it," Katherine said, avoiding eye contact with me. If she had looked at me while saying it, the statement would have meant one thing. When you say, "We're thinking about it" and smile and look into each other's eyes, it means you intend to reproduce. When you look straight ahead and avoid eye contact with your lover it means the topic is a point of contention. I wanted to have a kid, she didn't, that was our story, and sure I blamed the abortion for it. We'd even resisted getting officially married, ostensibly in protest that gay people couldn't get married, but mostly because the ceremony and psychological transformations involved really freaked us out. As Katherine put it, she didn't want to toss a whole meat and cheese tray off the bow of a boat just because someone brought the wrong nail polish remover.

The thermometer beeped and Julianne looked at the read-out. "Darling?" she said. "It appears I'm ovulating."

"It's not the spicy curry?" Bob said.

"I'm pretty sure not," Julianne said.

I couldn't tell whether this was supposed to be a hint that Katherine and I should leave. We picked at the edges of coasters swiped from a brew pub. Bob said, "Well I guess we should go upstairs and make a baby, then." We all laughed. Our friends rose from the couch.

"So yeah, we'll just take off," Katherine said.

"Oh no, no, we want you to stay," Julianne said. "I've been dying for a chance to play the new edition of Cranium. You guys stay put. This shouldn't take long at all."

"Not that, well, usually—" Bob said.

"There's Ben & Jerry's in the freezer," Julianne said as they hurried up the stairs. "Totally help yourselves."

Katherine and I sat on the couch. The master bedroom floor squeaked overhead. I finished the last smidge of my wine and said, "Maybe we should leave."

"We can't leave without saying goodbye," Katherine said. "That's rude."

"More rude than going off for a fuck while your friends hang out downstairs?"

"You won't believe what Julianne told me when you guys were down there playing guitar," Katherine said. "They placed one of those Internet ads looking for a woman to have a three way with. Can you believe that? I mean, this isn't college anymore."

25

"They said they have Ben & Jerry's," I said.

"Did you hear what I just said?"

"How am I supposed to react? Who cares? Good for them."

"They've had three women respond to it already."

"They've actually gone through with it?"

"Yeah! On the one hand trying to have a baby and on the other doing this sleazy Internet thing. Unbelievable."

We heard a couple squeaks of furniture upstairs and took that as a cue to move to the kitchen. I opened the freezer. "Looks like they have Chubby Hubby and Phish Food."

"How can you be so blasé about this?" Katherine asked. "These are our *friends*."

"What the hell's that supposed to mean?" I said.

"You are useless," Katherine said, genuinely disgusted. "Completely useless."

"You just wish they'd invited you into a three way," I said. "You already fucked Bob, you might as well go for Julianne, too."

This sort of petrified my girlfriend into a state of anger that neutralized her ability to think about ice cream. She walked briskly to the powder room with the fancy toilet paper holder and left me standing in the kitchen reading about bovine growth hormone. Wow, I'd played the you-fucked-Bob card. I hadn't done that in over a year. I wondered why I had chosen to play it tonight.

As promised, things seemed to conclude rather quickly upstairs. Bob, a little out of breath, now in sweatpants, joined me in the kitchen. "I see you found the ice cream. Julianne will be down in awhile. She's up there with her legs in the air trying to get my sperm to drip into her uterus. Hey, we have whipped cream and maraschino cherries if you guys want to do a sundae."

Katherine rejoined us and having known her for seven years I could tell she'd just suppressed a cry, probably with a terse, under-the-breath pep talk to the mirror with her angry, fluttering left eyelid. "I'll have a sundae," she said, "a really big one."

Dwelling on that water under the bridge between her and Bob, I wanted immediately to hurt her. I said, "Someone's gonna be doing a lot of Pilates tomorrow."

"I don't see you getting off your ass and exercising," Katherine said.

"Should I leave the room?" Bob laughed.

"Why, Bob, it's not like we're going to start screwing," Katherine said.

"Jesus, Kath," I said.

"No worries," Bob said. "You guys like nuts on your sundaes?"

"Sure thing," I said. "Lots of them."

Katherine excused herself, saying something about a board game. When she was out of earshot I said, "God, man, I'm sorry. I don't know what her deal is tonight."

"Yeah," Bob said, squirting a big pile of whipped cream on my sundae, finishing off the can. "Wanna do the whip-it?" he said, offering it to me.

"Sure," I said, taking the can from him. I emptied my lungs of air, put the nozzle in my mouth, then inhaled the remnants of nitrous oxide. My head tingled and felt about the size of one of those Mylar balloons you can buy at a county fair.

Bob said, "Things aren't *weird* are they?"

"Huh?"

"Like there's no weirdness. We're all cool with everything. Because it's really important to me that everything's cool. People's feelings and stuff."

"Yeah, Bob, everything's cool," I said, momentarily high. "Everything is so normal it's not even funny."

We brought the bowls of ice cream into the living room, where the women had set up the game on the coffee table. Julianne was wearing a bathrobe, her hair having assumed what the beauty industry called the just-fucked look. Bob fed her a maraschino. Katherine dug into her sundae as Bob assigned us pieces according to our favorite colors.

"Damn, I wish we had some pot," I said, which was another way of saying, "Hey Bob, got any pot?"

"I actually got some hash upstairs," Bob said.

"You still got that hookah from Egypt?"

"You know it."

"I thought we were going to play Cranium," Katherine said.

"Who's not playing?" I said.

"You can't smoke around Julianne," Katherine said, "not if she's pregnant."

"Oh yeah," I said.

"And if you guys go and smoke out, it's going to throw off the whole dynamic of the game," Katherine said, "two high people and two straight."

"The high team and the straight team doesn't work?" I said.

"Never mind, we don't have to smoke right now," Bob said, making the decision for the both of us, popping open the container of citrus-scented modeling clay.

We played one game all the way through, embarrassing ourselves with our fake enthusiasm, spelling words backwards, imitating Chuck Berry, trying to figure out how to convert a verb into a doodle. I knew that later that night I would enclose myself in my workroom with the *Monty Python* boxed set and a joint while Katherine pretended to sleep in the next room, and I wouldn't return to our bedroom until I was sure she had stopped crying.

"Some game," Bob said as he folded up the board.

"Yeah, well, it's getting late," Katherine said.

In the old days they would have begged us to stay longer but instead they told us it was time to leave by saying, "It was great seeing you guys." And so this palindrome of a dinner party ended with hugs and the saying of each others' names. Back in the Audi I turned the CD changer to Radiohead. Katherine waved to our friends, who stood on their slate entryway waving back at us. We left this street of $800K houses behind us and passed the lifestyle center, debating briefly about getting a DVD, deciding it was too late, as the car unconsciously found its way back to our garage. We sat inside listening to the end of a song until the motion sensor on the garage door opener decided we'd had enough light. In the darkness I asked Katherine if Bob knew she had aborted his baby. She said she'd been holding off telling him until he became a father.

Bee Beard

Bette wore the bee beard to work on a Tuesday. I typically arrive at the office before everyone else and had the place to myself. The card key scanner beeped, followed by Bette's heels on the parquet. At first I mistook the low buzzing for ambient noise from my computer monitor or a fluorescent light fixture. "Morning, Scott," Bette said, passing my cube. I mumbled back without looking up. The buzzing grew louder then trailed off as she headed down the hall. I groped for my cell thinking it was vibrating. A few moments of office time churned me through its routines.

Somebody else arrived, dragging latte smell past my cube. It was Bryce, our analytics maven, his actual title. At the other end of the hall Bryce punctured the quiet with a screech. I found him standing outside Bette's cube, his coffee dead and wet on the carpet. Bette wore what I had come to secretly call her Star Trek uniform, a hideous white suit jacket with too-pointy collars. From her face hung a beard of bees. Everyone's seen these things on TV or in *National Geographic*. Some farmer standing shirtless in his field, a stalactite of writhing insects dangling from his grinning face. But on Bette, though. Our account manager for digital media. I wasn't even aware she raised bees.

"You like?" she said, standing, pivoting in a circle. Bryce, often solicited for clothes-related opinions, was speechless, providing no fashion-oriented wisdom. Hot coffee steamed on the tips of his Diesel shoes.

"Aren't they going to miss their hive?" I said.

"Yeah, they'll want to eat, so I brought plenty of honey," Bette said.

"They're just going to stay on your face all day?" I said.

"Some of them will maybe want to fly around a little and check things out, but they should mostly stick with me."

"It's kind of like take your kids to work day," Bryce said.

"Right," I said. "Except with bees."

Our boss, Dan, five-plus years younger than all of us, appeared in the hallway, eyeballs-deep in a Powerpoint deck he was reviewing before our 9:30. "Whoa!" he said. "Who frickin' spilled the coffee?"

"Guilty!" Bryce said, picking up the cup, scooting to his desk.

"Scott. Bette. I made changes to slides 18 and 19. Let's hold on this Q3 long-range planning discussion. Bette, were you able to clear up that stuff with the streams and the error messages?"

Bette said, "Yeah. Turns out about four years ago they accepted a government grant contingent on a load of security measures. You know the flavor—total overkill with proxy servers, filters, firewalls. Their system was slowing things waaaaay down. Like twenty minutes for a 1.5MB .wav file to load. Good news is the agency that provided the grant was axed two years ago during budget cuts and the client is no longer stuck with their ridiculous architecture. I'm getting a consultation clause into the contract, which basically lets us spec out their program on their dime and ensure complete buy-off on platform integration."

Bryce bit his lower lip and raised his fist, knuckles facing away from his body, in an expression I had thoroughly analyzed. I theorized that he'd picked it up as a kid, from the stage behavior of certain heavy metal bands. Ideally, he should have been wearing studded gauntlets while making this gesture, which indicated a willingness to "rock," one of Bryce's favorite words. I had a subfolder where I saved emails in which he cited rocking as the primary measurement of success.

This team rocks!
Patty's presentation rocked.
Rock on, merchandisers.
I just want to publicly acknowledge that Program Manager Beth
    O'Grady truly rocked at today's 11:30.
Take a look at these FY04 actuals! They rock!!!
You thoroughly rock me, Help Desk.

But for all the supposed rocking, my job bored me most days, so I was happy someone had chosen to liven things up a bit by bringing a swarm of insects to the office. And Bette turned out to be right, they tended to stick close to her most of the day.

There were a couple mishaps. One of them got trapped inside the third floor break room snack machine. Another showed up on top of my monitor and proceeded to hump one of the Dungeons and Dragons figurines I keep up there as a joke, not because I'm seriously into Dungeons and Dragons. When Dot Simmons, one of our designers, received flowers because it was her birthday, the bees naturally freaked out and she had to stash the bouquet in her car the rest of the day. Overall, people were relatively accommodating. Once you got past the fear of being stung, it was pretty easy to carry on as usual with a person wearing a beard of bees.

Luckily, I found myself alone in the elevator with Bette at 6:30 that night. She leaned her head against the nicer wood than I have in my own house and said, "And what day is it? Only Tuesday? Gawd."

"No kidding."

"Do you have plans for dinner tonight?" Bette said.

"Is a can of minestrone a plan?"

We ended up at a new Thai restaurant where they made a big deal about customizing your sauce, a place bent on micromanaging the dining experience. I wondered how many hours of training the wait staff had endured. I imagined the Kinko'sed binders that must have been involved, the pep talks in the kitchen after which everyone clapped their hands together and repeated an inspirational phrase in unison.

"What's new in your life, Scott? Still learning Flash?"

The bees looked sluggish, occasionally dropping off Bette's face onto the table, then feebly flying back to join their fellow bees.

"Nah, but I've been taking a class at the community college on this DVD authoring software that's pretty great. Someday everything you see in theaters is going to be made in people's garages on their computers. It'll be awesome. What about you? I guess beekeeping?"

"You should see my place. The hives. It's gotten a little out of control," Bette laughed. I knew what this laugh meant. It meant, no really, you should see my place. I'm serious. Like, tonight.

"You thinking of getting out of digital media and raising bees full time?"

"Oh no," she said. "Beekeeping is just sort of a side thing."

"Kind of hard in a condo, I'd imagine."

"So Scott, what I really wanted to—"

The waiter arrived with our customized sauces and spring rolls. Only when he knew that we were satisfied with the proportions of sauce ingredients did he step away to help other patrons.

"You were saying," I said.

"Dan gave his notice today."

"You're kidding. Dan?"

"Yeah. He got this big offer from Versatech. Like twice his salary, four weeks' vacation. Offers, counter-offers, they've been going back and forth for weeks."

"I would have never known. He seemed so dialed in today. What's this mean for you?"

Bette shrugged and smiled, as if to say she already knew she was lined up for Dan's position. Which would make her my boss. Which indicated that I should really initiate the sexual relationship now, before the annual review period, to avoid violating the quid pro quo section of the *Sexual Harassment: It's No Joking Matter* manual.

Then I got stung. I must have moved my silverware in a threatening manner. I felt this wicked needle on the back of my hand. There was the bee, its thorax bent in an obscene posture, pumping its venom into me. Goddamn it hurt. The bee left the stinger in my flesh then wobbled off toward the customized sauce to live out its final moments. Bette apologized and fished a dwindling cube from her glass, which she rubbed across the quickly swelling spot.

"I'm so sorry," Bette said. "This is embarrassing."

"No worries," I said. "Damn that hurts. I haven't been stung by a bee since . . . I guess I can't ever remember being stung by a bee. Wow. So this Dan situation."

"So last year at my review I talked to him about potentially taking on radio and print as well as digital media and he seemed to really encourage the idea."

"Wow, that's—" I started coughing. "That's fantastic."

"You've drank all your water. Here, have some of mine."

As I was reaching for Bette's glass the entire restaurant appeared to implode, as though I were inside a balloon in the process of having the air sucked out of it. I couldn't breathe and naturally panicked, jerking my arms and inadvertently knocking the spring rolls to the floor, which was where I ended up as well. I didn't have the presence of mind to know I was having a severe allergic reaction to the bee sting. This was explained to me later, in the emergency room. By the time I'd made it to the hospital I was covered in hives, my eyes burned, I was wheezing, and my hand looked like an infielder's mitt. The admitting desk wouldn't let Bette into the emergency room because of her bees and suggested that she hang out with the smoking nurses by the ambulance bay. I was in there for a couple hours, getting shots of antihistamines and learning I was one of those rare people who can die from a single sting. After receiving the bee sting brochure and thanking the doctor, I found Bette sitting on a landscape boulder, reading *Lucky: The Magazine About Shopping* under a parking lot light while her insects slept.

"You didn't have to wait for me," I said.

"I feel somewhat responsible for this."

"I feel bad you waited. It's almost midnight."

"Let me drive you back to your car."

"It's not far, I can walk."

"You can't walk. It's too late."

"I'll call a cab."

"Really, Scott—"

"I'm just a little uncomfortable about the bees right now. Apparently about 1 percent of the population is severely allergic to bee venom, and I'm in the 1 percent within that 1 percent that can apparently die from a sting."

"Okay. I understand."

I had started the evening sexually attracted to Bette and I was ending it sort of hating her. Not because one of her bees had stung me, per se—who could have predicted my immune system would react the way it had—but because I knew she was going to take Dan's place on the team and become my boss, and that this bungled pseudo date had 86'd my chances of ever getting her in the sack. Word of my trip to the emergency room would somehow get out, I was sure, because Bette—as she'd demonstrated sharing this Dan development with me—was a notorious gossip. When everyone found out about the incident they'd naturally wonder why we'd gone out to dinner together, construe it as an actual—not pseudo—date and then know I had failed to get it on with the new director of digital media.

The next morning Bette had the audacity to show up to work with her damn bee beard again, which was even longer than it had been the day before. If ZZ Top had pursued beekeeping careers instead of becoming Texas blues rockers, they would have looked like Bette. I checked my Outlook calendar and discovered she was in my subscription email strategy meeting at 3 P.M. I arrived purposely on time and sat as far away from her as I could. Laksmi, the developer who was supposed to be showing us the new templates, struggled with the projector. We tried to offer her technical support:

"Is the cable plugged in?"

"Hit enter."

"Did you hit powersave?"

"Try unplugging it and plugging it back in."

"Hit enter again."

"Is the lens cap still on?"

When Laksmi finally had the presentation projected in a trapezoidal shape on the irregularly shaped wall, the bees went a little crazy with the sudden change in light, butting their heads into the pie charts like they were flowers. Bette's beard began to sag, misshapen, bees crawling over her shoulders and arms onto the table and leftover handouts from the previous meeting. Laksmi made a joke about the bees thinking the projector was sunlight.

"Is it just me," I said, "or does it maybe seem like a good idea for people to leave their pets at home."

"I thought we had a dog-friendly policy," Laksmi said.

"I'm not talking about the friendly dog policy. I'm talking about bees. Bette's bees. Bette, I don't know, maybe it's not kosher to bring them to work? Am I out of line suggesting this?"

Bette squeezed out a withering glance and made some reference to the employee manual.

"Maybe I wasn't paying much attention or something during orientation," I said, "but I don't recall seeing a section on bringing your hive to work."

"Let's take this offline," Bette said, which is a more productive sounding way of saying, "Let's talk about this later." I found it impossible to concentrate the rest of the meeting. Immediately afterward, we found the office of some guy who'd been laid off and closed the door behind us. "You have a problem with my work?" Bette said.

"Jesus, Bette, this isn't about work. It's about me being afraid of going into anaphylactic shock. I honor diversity as much as anyone around here; I've even got the special certificate to prove it. But this is out of line. I don't know what the solution is. I just know your bees present a health risk to me and I wish you'd stop to consider that."

"This isn't about health risks at all, Scott. You've wanted Dan's position since the day you started here. You can't stand the idea of me stepping into his shoes. You're looking for any angle you can to make me look bad."

"You are so full of shit."

"I saw how you reacted when I told you he gave his notice. As if you don't think seniority means they owe you the position. Fuck that. We're up 79 percent YTD in digital media sales because of the initiatives I've driven. What have you owned? Some piece-of-shit animations for the home page that drive no sales? Give me a fucking break."

"I don't understand why you're so angry, Bette. I thought we were friends."

She settled down a bit and leaned against the laid off guy's desk. On the desk were an open can of Diet Coke and a half-eaten Krispy Kreme resting on an upside down paper cup— Pompeii-like remnants of the day the poor sucker got the axe. One of her bees flew off her face and landed on my shirt sleeve.

"Get it off, get it off, get it off."

Bette used the paper cup to gently remove the bee from my shirt and reintroduce it to her chin.

"It's because I've fallen for you, Bette. You know that."

"There, you finally said it."

"Did you have to get angry to get it out of me?"

"I never thought you were going to admit it is all."

"I was going to talk to you about it last night but, you know, the bee sting."

Bette drew closer and touched my arm. "I've wanted you, it's true."

"I want to kiss you, Bette," I said, pulling away, "but the bees."

"Okay," she sighed. "Tomorrow I'll leave them at home. For you."

The next day, true to her word, Bette stopped by my cube sans bees. She offered me an Altoid from her Kate Spade bag and said she was sorry about the day before. "I said some things I didn't mean. You're a really great friend and I want to keep it that way. Your Flash animations are really cool, I mean it."

"No worries," I said, "I know how crazy it can get here. And I hope—Well I was thinking if you're free this weekend—"

"We'll see," Bette said. "We'll see."

Fifteen minutes later I was retrieving some prints from the copy room when I heard that dreaded buzzing again. Then Dan walked in. "What up, Scott? That my print job there? No? Sorry man, I'm a little out of it this morning. Late night, if you know what I mean," he said, his face dripping with bees.

Blood Relatives

I. My Mother Was a Monster

I followed my mother's legs through the glistening aisles of Albertson's as she selected items for the Wednesday night meal. We were usually Spaghettios-level people, a Hamburger Helper family. We opened our main courses with can openers and dumped the contents into microwave-safe crockery. Our fingernails ripped the glued cardboard seams of boxes that invariably contained "seasoning packets." Most nights my mother dumped upon our table all manner of instant foods, stuff designed to be cooked inside a plastic bag, blobs of starchy substance molten around the edges and frozen solid in the center. To preserve what little domestic dignity she retained, Mom had declared that every Wednesday night we would eat what she called "the fancy meal."

I was the only one among my siblings my mother tolerated as a grocery shopping partner. It was my responsibility to lobby on my brother and sister's behalf for things we actually wanted to eat. While the nutritional value of our lunches and dinners was always suspect, my parents still held firm to a principle they had established during a brief health food flirtation in the seventies— *no sugared cereal*. I steeled myself as we rolled into the cereal aisle, where cartoon characters taunted me from their boxes, pimping the secret prizes within.

I selected a box of Honeycomb, affecting an expression of malnourished need. My mom flattened her wide lips and shook her First Lady hairdo.

"But Mom," I said, "it's *a delicious part of this nutritious breakfast.*"

"Since you and your brother and sister did such a good job cleaning the garage I'll let you splurge and get Frosted Mini-Wheats."

Fuck. Frosted Mini-Wheats hardly counted as sugared cereal. I could hear my sister miming a gag, my brother denouncing it as "fag cereal." I switched tactics and decided to ask for more than I expected, hoping that I could steer my mom to the center, to something like Honey Nut Cheerios. I pulled down a box of Captain Crunch.

"Not in a million years. You'll rot your face out. It's either Mini-Wheats or you're getting Grape Nuts."

"Crispy Wheats and Raisins?"

"*Patrick.*"

"Okay. Frosted Mini-Wheats."

We lived in the kind of neighborhood every American should be familiar with by now. Kids throwing newspapers from bikes? Check. Shirtless man with hairy nipples on front porch waving to the mailman? Check. Teenage dude blasting Judas Priest from his

GTO? Misogynistic signage on a tree house? Lady with a big butt gardening in mismatching yellow plaids? Check, check, check.

My brother and sister, Greg and Yvonne, bore down on the station wagon to paw through the groceries as soon as we pulled into the driveway. Yvonne quickly located her feminine items and hid them inside her sweatshirt. Greg scrutinized his canister of muscle bulking powder upon which an oiled wall of musculature flexed. Here's everything you need to know about my siblings: they were both in high school, had both had sex with their respective partners in our basement rec room (when the rest of us weren't home), and had both told me about these experiences in graphic detail.

"Quit digging through the bags, just get everything inside!" my mom said. My mom's name was Lorraine, and she looked like a Lorraine. Sometimes you see people who look so much like their names it's as though their features conformed to whatever their parents decided to call them. On the other hand, I felt I had been poorly named. For years I had been trying to convince my parents to let me legally change my name from Patrick to Lars. Watching a show on transsexuals one night, I suddenly understood: I was a Lars trapped in the name of a Patrick.

Greg was openly breaking one of the rules of the household— no heavy metal on the living room stereo. My mom hissed at him to turn it off, which struck me as ironic; the song presently vibrating the Hummel figurines perched on the speakers was about authority figures who don't appreciate the need to party on overdrive. With the plastic bags sagging on the kitchen island, Greg quickly located the offensive box of cereal and squinted cruelly at me. "Hey, Patrick, check it out. Did you know that Frosted Mini-Wheats are really popular in San Francisco? Know what I mean? San Francisco?"

We proceeded to slap fight. Greg put me in a headlock and hissed into my ear, "Your choice. My armpit or my fart. I'm giving you three seconds to decide which one to smell. Armpit or fart."

"Greg, just put away the darn groceries. Patrick, go check on the main course."

I wiggled out of my brother's grip, got in one good slap, then trudged down to the basement and opened the freezer. I had left it propped open with a can of tuna so Carl could get some air and had given him one of my windbreakers so he wouldn't get too cold. Still, I found the kid shivering and sniffling, sitting on bags of frozen peas and carrots, eating a freezer-burnt Halloween cookie in the shape of a witch hat. Carl was in my grade and played goalie on my soccer team, a position he had attained through sheer nepotism, since his dad was the coach.

"W-what are you d-doing?" Carl said.

"Shut up, Carl. Now listen, okay? I happen to know my mom wants to make you for dinner, but we're all hoping for pizza pockets instead. She makes crummy stews."

Carl started crying again and I had to put my hand over his mouth to ensure his pleas for mercy couldn't be heard up through the laundry chute. A toilet flushed upstairs; my dad was home. The walls of the basement reverberated with the ambient noise of moving sewage.

"When you hear the toilet flush two times, that's your signal that it's okay to escape. Just go up the stairs and turn left, go out the back porch and make sure the door doesn't slam shut. You're going to have to wade across the creek to the woods, then head toward the high school. You should be safe by the time you reach it. And run fast. My mom did track and field in college."

Carl nodded. I returned upstairs, my stomach growling as I imagined the gooey interior of a combo-flavored pizza pocket.

My dad, guy by the name of Dean, worked at a local factory that made crayons, doing something he called "Planning Guidelines." At barbecue-like events he would brag that he had "put pressure on top management" to change the name of the "flesh" crayon. All we knew was that when they fucked up a color, we got the rejects. Today there had been a mistake with a batch of red-orange; it had come out too much like orange-red. Several misshapen bricks of this color sat on the dining room table.

My father and I performed our eight-part secret handshake. "Patrick, my man. What did they rot your brain with in school today?"

"Photosynthesis," I said.

"Hey, that's cool. Well if you need to use my camera, just lemme know." My dad swept my mother up in his arms and twirled her around the kitchen. "Lorraine my dear! Let's forget about inept pigment technicians who can't tell the difference between Yellow #8 and Orange #3, okay? I'm starving. What's for dinner?"

"His name is Carl," my mom said.

I fell to the kitchen linoleum clutching my side and cried out. "Patrick, what happened? What is it?" my mother said.

"Oh my God . . . appendix . . . rupturing . . . the pain. . . . "

My mom palpated my abdomen then helped me to the up-stairs bathroom. I kind of pretended to fall against the toilet and accidentally flush it. Groaning, I flailed my arms around and pre-tended to accidentally flush it again. My mom stood over me with her hands on her hips. I imagined Carl climbing out of the freezer with Halloween-colored cookie sprinkles on his lips, shivering in my windbreaker, ascending the stairs. I heard the back screen door slam shut. An expression of panic must have passed over me. My mom scowled and said, "Hey, what's going on here?"

Yvonne screeched from her room and raced to join us. "Oh my god mom, I totally saw Carl running across our yard."

My mother growled at me. "There will be consequences," she said, then fetched one of her axes from behind the toilet bowl. "Well are you just going to sit there stupidly, or are you going to help me get that little snot-nosed jerk?"

Dusk had begun to overtake our backyard, but I was able to see Carl escaping through the trees on the other side of the creek. I should have lent him my camo jacket. Holding the axe aloft, my mother led us on a chase for our supper. I managed to keep up for the most part, while my brother surged ahead and my dad and sister lagged behind. I knew Carl wasn't swift on his feet; there was a reason our team was in last place in our division. I just hoped he could make it to the high school. While I dreaded the prospect of a dinner of Carl, I found myself sort of admiring my mother as she leapt over fallen trees and hacked her way through sticker bushes in pursuit of her quarry. I certainly couldn't imagine David Thompson's or Nick Peterson's moms wielding an axe at full speed through the woods without getting a single snag in their panty hose. My brother, showing off his tight end skills, tackled Carl and pinned him to the forest floor. Soon we were standing in a semicircle, breathing hard, staring into the terrified eyes of the worst goalie I had ever known. My mother raised her axe. The muscles in her neck tightened and her eyes went unnaturally wide as she bellowed a war cry. The noise should have been recorded and used as a sound effect for a movie about a bunch of people who attack each other and stuff. Yes indeed, birds rose from trees into the sky upon hearing it, signifying impending terror.

My dad loudly cleared his throat. "Now Lorraine, let's just think this through a little bit here."

My mother's death-blow wail pathetically trailed off, like a safe and sane sparkling cone firework. My dad gently pried the axe from her hands and put his arm around her shoulder. I knew then that a man with guts enough to call a crayon racist was a man who could dissuade my mother from cannibalism.

"We love your cooking, honey, it's just . . . we're kind of tired of fancy night."

"Is it how I prepare them? I can try a different recipe."

Greg helped Carl to his feet. "You don't have to impress us with your cooking, Mom," he said.

"We like the instant stuff better," I said.

"So are you like going to kill him or what?" my sister said.

I sneered back at her. "Are you crazy? Why kill someone for dinner when there's pizza pockets and mini drumstick bites at home?"

"Hey, here's an idea," my dad said. "Let's let Carl go so he can continue his goalie duties on Patrick's team."

"Yeah, let him go so they can suck another day," Greg said, frowning at me, pointing to his armpit, his ass, his nose.

Carl sprinted, crying, through the woods toward the high school. My mother called plaintively after him, "Carl, honey, be sure to tell your mother I have something I want to donate to the YWCA raffle."

As we walked home, I could tell my sister was a little disappointed we weren't having fancy night. My brother and dad reenacted football plays from mythic games, leaping over exposed roots and mossy stumps with pretend footballs tucked under their arms. I asked my mother if I could carry the axe. Sounding worn out, she said sure, and handed it to me. I took a couple swings at some randomly selected trees and ran my finger down the worn handle, where she had cut a number of notches with a pocket knife, each notch representing a fancy night.

I had assumed we would have pizza pockets in lieu of Carl for dinner that night, but I had assumed wrong. My mother still held me accountable for the meal that got away, and as punishment assigned me the purposeless task of sweeping the basement. I pushed the broom back and forth across the concrete, my stomach growling forlornly. All the embarrassing phases my family had undergone were on display down here, a graveyard of exercise machines, a karaoke unit with a microphone repaired with layers of duct tape. The beaten down couch, where my brother and sister had laid their respective mates. The ancient TV with the enigmatic UHF dial and an antenna you had to wiggle to catch a signal. A floor-to-ceiling stack of cartons of discontinued, Caucasian-resembling crayons. I listened to my family chatter and laugh upstairs and fantasized that they had forgotten I even existed. I would live down here while they went about the business of eating healthy cereal and watching nature documentaries on TV. I could live down here for years, sleep on the couch, subsist on frozen cookie dough, draw some beige things, get a lot of exercise.

My mother opened the door to the basement, interrupting my train of thought. "Patrick, when you're done sweeping, could you pick out some leftovers to bring up?"

I said sure, and leaned the broom against the wall. The freezer was still open from Carl's escape. I peered inside at all the foil-wrapped packages, the ones labeled with names of kids I used to know, wondering what sounded good for dinner.

This story was inspired by a work of art by Raymond Pettibon.

II. Profession

It was Dads Day at my six-year-old's kindergarten class. We sat in miniature chairs arranged in a semicircle on the rug, answering questions about our professions. One dad drove a beer truck, another was a landscape architect. There were two orthopedic surgeons among us. The teacher, Ms. Vanderbilt, nodded at me when it was my turn.

"I'm a serial killer."

"Pardon?" Ms. Vanderbilt said.

"I murder people. Maybe you've seen some of the books about me." I withdrew from my Discovery Channel tote bag a number of paperbacks chronicling my career.

A boy in the back raised his hand. "What kind of people do you kill?" he said.

"Nobody important," I said, and the room seemed to come down several notches, terror-wise.

Ms. Vanderbilt seemed intent on challenging me, or making me an example of bad career choices. "So can you actually make a decent living as a serial murderer?"

"You can make," I paused a beat, "a *killing*." A couple of the dads reacted audibly to the pun.

I was hyper-aware that my son, Kenny, might be embarrassed. He had expressed some anxiety the night before that my line of work wasn't as "cool" as those of some of the other dads. But he beamed at the reaction I got when I passed around the McFarlane Toys action figure that had been molded in my likeness, albeit with more musculature.

"When you get good enough at something," I explained, "you can become what is known as a consultant. Like Mr. Nakayama here, who works on computers."

"Actually, I'm a private contractor," Gary Nakayama said. "Sorry to interrupt. There is a difference."

"At any rate," I continued, "there are always people interested in paying money for your time when you have particular, specialized skills. For instance, I have recently been contacted by a crime writer who wants to run her manuscript by me to see if she got the details right."

"What kinds of weapons do you use?" Kenny, my ringer, asked from the front row.

"It really depends. Generally rope or a knife."

"Do you ever use a gun?" a little girl said.

"I don't like guns," I said. "Too noisy. And by the way, do all of you know what to do if you find a gun?"

"*Tell an adult*," they said in unison.

"Thank you, Mr. Davis," Ms. Vanderbilt said. "Moving along. Well it looks like Mr. Delbanco has brought along one of his friends from the animal hospital!"

I make dinner on Wednesday nights, that's the arrangement I have with Carol, my wife. Sometimes Kenny joins me, helps me make the salad or put melted garlic butter on the bread. His older brother, Milt, typically spends his evenings in his room listening to rap metal, and tonight was no exception. Luckily, Kenny was at an age when dad-son activities were fun.

"I hope I did all right," I said. "I hope I didn't embarrass you today."

"It was okay," Kenny said, and I took this as high praise.

"When I was your age I was embarrassed that my dad was a plumber. But when I got a little older I understood that hey, plumbers take care of important things."

"Is what you do important?"

I shrugged. "Depends on how you look at it, doesn't it, Kenny? The people I kill are generally lower class. You know, the types of people who pee at the bus stop and yell at each other in the street. So in the sense that the world could use a lot fewer of those people, then sure, I guess you could say what I do is important."

Carol clicked into the kitchen in her fancier-type shoes, one of her CPR dummies under her arm. "Can you help me load these guys into the minivan?" she said. I didn't have the heart to tell her there was a flake of what appeared to be basil adhered to one of her front teeth. She taught classes at the community college and usually ran behind. I helped her carry the rubber torsos from the living room to the family vehicle, strapping the multiculturally pigmented dummies into their seats.

"I love you," I said, kissing her, "more than you can ever know."

"Are you working tonight?" Carol said.

"Yeah, I think I will."

"Well make sure to get Kenny's jammies from the dryer before you put him to bed."

"I've got it all taken care of, Chief," I said. As my wife turned the van around she backed over some bad landscaping we won at a charity auction. I watched her speed out of the cul-de-sac, off to teach people how to prevent their loved ones from choking to death.

I knocked on Milt's door, which was ajar. Something staccato and threatening played on his computer speakers. I found him reading a book propped up on the keyboard. Lit by a desk lamp, as if on display, was a neat row of toenail clippings apparently arranged according to size.

"Howdy pardner," I said. "What you reading there?"

"Michel Foucault."

"Woman writer, huh?" I said, realizing I was going down a conversational dead end. "So say I was planning on going out for a while tonight. I was wondering if you could take care of your brother until bedtime and get him all settled in."

"Sure, whatever."

"And by taking care of him I mean not just leaving your door open. Maybe you guys can play a game together, or color."

"Color?"

"I'm not suggesting *you* would be doing any coloring. I'm just saying that you could maybe supervise and provide some positive feedback during a coloring activity."

"Okay."

"Milt?"

"Yeah?"

"Are you gay?"

"Jesus, Dad."

"Because if you are, just let us know. Your mom and I would be happy to join one of those organizations. Flag-wavers or whatever they call it."

"You made your point. I'll watch Kenny. Please leave me alone."

"Now is that any way to, uh, talk to your—"

"I said 'please.'"

"Right. Yeah. I'll be going."

I was actually glad to be dismissed by my son. My thoughts had turned to prostitutes' necks, the bulging veins of their temples, their sickening strip mall perfumes. Carol likened my killing cycle to her menstrual cycle, even called it my "male period." I hurriedly got Kenny into his jammies, told him jokingly to watch his brother for me, and revved up my restored black Trans Am with the phoenix detailing on the hood. My cozy neighborhood hawked me up and spit me out in a cloud of carbon monoxide into mixed-use commercial zones with flickering plastic reader boards and balloons sagging from espresso stand clapboards. I cruised the strip: Chevron, Speedy Lube, Kentucky Fried Chicken, AM/PM, North Shore Title and Escrow. I considered the easy kill of a drunk passed out at a bus stop, but that seemed cheap. I was about to grab a decaf mocha and call it a night when I spotted a known transvestite hooker standing on the corner of 22nd and Bellmont. I pulled over.

"Hi beautiful," I said, "you looking for a boyfriend?"

We drove to an abandoned construction site near the bridge. The funding had dried up for this project; skeletal columns of rebar rose from what had been envisioned as an office park.

"Let's do it in the back," I said. "There's more room. Hold on. That door only opens from the outside. I'll let you out."

After I had helped her out of the car and she had turned her back, I rammed my knife into a soft spot beneath her right shoulder blade. She turned into a statistic. She reached out and steadied herself on the roof of the car as I pulled the knife out and stabbed her under the ribs.

"Let me see your eyes, let me see your eyes," I panted, turning her around. She stared at me, bewildered with pain, unable to speak through a mouth full of blood. Her arms were flapping spaghetti noodles that were no match for my bench-press-conditioned upper body.

"I am your sweet fucking angel of death, cunt!" I screamed into her face. One, two, three more stabs and life abandoned her.

I wrapped the body in a plastic tarp, tying off the ends so it wouldn't leak, then drove a half hour out of town to the abandoned drive-in theater. I deposited it behind the screen in a patch of stinging nettles. With some Armor All wipes I cleaned the blood off the car and drove home listening to a radio call-in show where two personalities lamely debated a new transportation tax bill.

I got home well after midnight and parked the car next to Carol's minivan, letting myself in through the garage entrance so I could deposit my stained clothes in the hamper before heading up to bed. In my boxers, I tiptoed through the kitchen, stopping and gasping as I rounded the corner to the living room. Silhouettes of six individuals were waiting for me. I flipped on the dimmer and found Carol's CPR dummies arranged on the furniture. I hated when she did this to me. Another one of her jokes. How much is it to ask that a man not be deliberately terrified in his own home?

Drugs and Toys

We at Halstein's Drugs care about our customers. I realize that this bold statement immediately puts me in the company of so many other businesses who profess a commitment to customer service but who don't live up to it. But this drugstore has supported my family for four generations and if we hadn't cared about our customers we would have been swallowed by the likes of Rite Aid and Walgreens long ago. We could have been one of those unwashed storefronts with grimy merchandise pathetically fading into oblivion. An out-of-date name in someone's ancient Yellow Pages. Last year's newspaper duct taped to the windows. A retail casualty.

You might find it odd that a company that traffics in remedies for maladies of the most discreet nature is so candid about customers' intimate needs. Within the borders of the human body there are places so fetid and ugly that it seems impossible to us that other people harbor such pimpled wrinkles and smelly crevices. Infected follicles appear beneath our clothing. In private moments we inspect the irregularities of our skin pigmentation. After we have made ourselves presentable we step from our bathrooms into the rest of humanity, this gleaming parade of appearances, where skin is buffed to a healthy-looking sheen and hair is conditioned with moisture-locking beads for deep-penetrating, revitalizing action. We at Halstein's live behind the veil of how people hope they appear. We accept illness and imperfection as the cost of the awesome miracle that we have found ourselves here on earth inhabiting physical forms. We see our customers as they truly are, and we've stayed in business all these years because we love them that way, unconditionally.

When Vera Barker comes into the store, my thoughts turn to the polyp she found in her armpit the previous week. Not only do I know that Dylan McCormack has head lice, I know that he came down with it during wrestling practice and that he ended up winning the tournament in his weight class. There's a guy who comes in every month and picks up a particular brand of imported German toothpaste. His name is Gary and he runs a graphic design business that is barely getting by in this depressed economy. I know that when Gary's business finally goes under and he is down to his last eight dollars, he will sooner spend it on that tube of Meridol than on food.

Last week Gary parked across the street and before he even made it to the door, I had his toothpaste waiting for him on the counter.

"How's the design business, Gary?" I said. Small talk, certainly, but such banter builds customer loyalty.

"Lousy," Gary said, "and I'll take a box of Camel Light 100s."

"Soft pack again?"

"That's fine, Bud."

I rang Gary up and that was the extent of our transaction. Later that evening I called him at his home studio, where he works well into the night. "Hi Gary. It's Bud at Halstein's. I hope I didn't catch you at a bad time. I know you work late, so I figured I'd call and see how that toothpaste is treating you."

"I haven't brushed with it yet."

"That's okay, I'll wait."

"Thanks," Gary said. He set down the phone. I faintly heard running water. A minute later he came back. "There. Just used it. It's great stuff as always."

"Good to hear, Gary. You still using the Butler G-U-M medium bristle?"

"Yeah, why?"

"I think you're due for a new one. You got the one with the replacement heads, if I'm not mistaken. Those should have worn out by now."

"Hey, thanks for the reminder. I'll pick one up the next time I'm in."

When Halstein's acquires new customers, we retain them for life. Take Margaret Vance, who's been shopping with us for ten years. I remember when she first came in looking for a roll of assorted fruit-flavored Tums. We didn't have any in stock, but I sold her an off-brand antacid that she still religiously puts in her basket every time she shops. Nowadays that basket is always brimming with shampoos and eye drops and nail polish remover. I know the medical history of her extended family like a series of prayers. And I know she is sensitive about dandruff. Halstein's is the kind of place where you can feel safe opening up on such subjects. I remember sitting on the counter as a child listening to my grandfather's discourse on the color of a customer's stool. We are allowed to speak of such topics in this sacred place we call the drugstore because here physical inadequacy is treated as a universal truth to which each of us must humbly bow. And the well-timed sales and special offers keep them on their toes, as well.

Last month I made a big mistake and neglected to put Ms. Vance's special conditioner in the bag. Beside myself with visions of the young lady being unable to wash and rinse as she was accustomed, I closed the shop early and drove across town to her condominium. She was making dinner when I rang and graciously invited me in. Apologizing that the eggplant parmesan she had prepared was but a single serving, she offered me a glass of soda water that I humbly accepted. While I watched her eat we got to talking about the best way to treat athlete's foot, which she had picked up at the racquetball court. I was familiar with a number of products, but when you got down to brass tacks, Pro Clearz Brush-On Antifungal Liquid was the product I trusted most. She thanked me, and then there was an awkward moment when she had finished her dinner.

"Say," Ms. Vance said, "since you're here, would you be interested in hanging out with me while I wash my hair?"

"I would be delighted," I said. Ms. Vance led me to the bathroom where I sat on the toilet while she disrobed. I view the private places in the human body with the utmost clinical maturity, and the only pleasure I received from witnessing Ms. Vance's hygienic ritual was purely professional. Her body became fuzzed out behind the translucent glass door of the shower like a defendant scrambled on Court TV. She let me peek up over the top to watch the application of her hair care products. She used three different types of shampoo and an herbal scalp treatment followed by two cycles of conditioner. I handed her a towel when she emerged forty minutes later and could barely restrain myself from applauding. Her ingenious combination of hair cleansing and rejuvenating products left me duly impressed.

You see, I learn as much from my customers as they learn from me. Any old clerk can recommend particular brands of shaving cream, but it takes an active listener to understand that an African American man's beard has different needs than that of a Caucasian or Asian man.

Of course the most sensitive matters are sexual in nature. Our family planning aisle is located discreetly in the back of the store, next to orthopedics. When a person who looks much too young to be engaged in sexual intercourse purchases condoms or spermicidal jelly, I treat him the same as the couples in their late twenties who seek my guidance on male fertility tests. I believe unwaveringly that decisions related to sexuality are the province of individuals and their partners, and I remove myself entirely from purchasing decisions unless my expertise is called upon. Such was the case with Jason Gilroy, a young man whose career as a prosecuting attorney had begun to flower owing to a couple decisive victories in very public cases. I have known him practically his whole life, from the days when he used to buy comic books and Bazooka gum. Now that he is preoccupied with more adult concerns, I have found that we can speak man to man. Jason has had a fair number of girl-friends as well as occasional homosexual encounters. I pass no judgment on such affairs. If I am asked to expound upon the ideal lubricants for varying orifices, it is within my professional capacity to do so. More often than not, however, I give Jason advice on our selection of higher-end men's skin care and hair loss remedies. Recently Jason walked into the store with his new girlfriend, to whom I was promptly introduced.

"An absolute pleasure," I said to the tall, brunette woman named Holly. She was as pretty as the women in a Sunday cosmetics circular.

"Bud here takes care of me," Jason said, "He can cure anything."

I laughed. "No, no. The drug companies do the research and development, I am merely a purveyor of their products."

"Good tip on the night-time cough medicine," Jason said. "Thanks to your advice I was able to get a good night's sleep before that trial. And guess what—I nailed that half-million dollars for my client."

"Whatever I can do to help," I said, then squinted at Holly. "Is that a stye on your lower left eyelid?"

"Excuse me?" Holly said, pulling her head back.

"Here, come closer. That little pimple on your eyelid. An inflamed swelling of the sebaceous gland. I bet it hurts."

"Don't worry, Holly," Jason said, "Bud knows what he's doing."

"I just think it's a little personal."

Jason and I both laughed this time. Jason said, "Nothing in Halstein's is too personal, babe."

"Well, okay," Holly said, and cautiously brought her head closer to mine so I could inspect the stye.

"Whatever you do, you're going to have to let it get absorbed on its own, but I have a little something that will speed up the process and make it less painful," I said. "The pus inside a stye is filled with viruses that can lead to more styes. You don't want to get into a vicious cycle of popping styes and getting new ones."

While I retrieved the eye drops in question, Jason picked up some soap and mouthwash.

"By the way," I said, "your pictures came back." I handed Jason an envelope of glossies. "I saw that you have been documenting your romantic liaisons. I was a little surprised to see some depictions of intercourse without a condom."

"Oh, I'm on the pill," Holly said.

"It wasn't you in the pictures," I said. "Still, it's not a bad idea to get in the habit of using barrier protection. You don't know where each other have been, and this early in your relationship it's better to be safe than sorry."

Jason threw up his hands and shook his head. "Right again. I'll try to be better about that, Bud, I promise."

"You two lovebirds have a great rest of the afternoon."

Halstein's has occupied the same storefront for sixty years. My father bought the building at a time when he had enough cash in the bank to move the place to a wealthier neighborhood. I've seen this part of town thrive and fall into disrepair, but we have remained loyal to our customer base and they have kept us in the black in the worst

71

of times. About ten years ago, this historic district of brick slaughterhouses and cobbled sidewalks began a slow resurgence. Artists priced out of downtown set up their studios and coffee shops. Then the neighborhood started attracting more young couples and curious out-of-towners and I saw a little spike in our daily sales. I have seen businesses come and go over the years—used bookstores, dog grooming salons, pizza joints, video stores—and through it all, Halstein's has remained the anchor of the local business community.

Then a new business started moving into a small storefront across the street. While sipping my morning coffee I watched movers push hand trucks laden with boxes of merchandise through the double doors. In the spirit of strengthening community ties, I walked across the street to introduce myself. I spotted a slightly boxy-looking woman with split ends but a real natural glow to her complexion who seemed to be directing the moving operation.

"Bud Halstein, Halstein's Drug. Welcome to the neighborhood!"

"Yeah. I'm Jeaneane. Uh, this is Miramack Wholesale Toys."

"Toys!" I said. "It's been years since we had a toy store in the neighborhood! Fantastic."

"Yeah, well we're not—Never mind. Nice meeting you, I guess."

I could see Jeaneane was occupied with her move—she was surely paying these gentlemen by the hour—so I left her alone and spent the rest of the morning replenishing the magazines and thinking of things I could put in a welcome basket to make Miramack feel more at home.

Jeaneane and her crew worked through the weekend to set up shop. I offered to help but was rebuffed. She had it all under control. A plain white sign went up, nothing special but handsomely crafted. Bins of brightly colored stuffed animals and balls and costumes were artfully laid out, and an electric train set was arranged in the display window. Once in a while I would catch Jeaneane with her hands on her hips, frowning in thought as she gazed out the window, but she never returned my waves. She seemed to have no interest in visiting Halstein's, but I didn't fault her for that. She was a businesswoman with a demanding schedule, so it was probably best we kept our distance for the time being.

On the first day Miramack was open, I watched a young woman with her son, who looked to be about eight years old, gaze excitedly into the storefront at all the toys inside. It always warms my heart to see a fledgling enterprise greeted with such enthusiasm from its brand-new customers. I have been known to get misty-eyed gazing upon framed first dollars in restaurants. At any rate, the young woman and her son entered Miramack Toys and I returned to the article in *American Pharmacist* that I'd been reading. When I looked up again, I saw the young woman and her son with Jeaneane on the sidewalk outside Miramack's. The little guy was crying fiercely, rubbing his eyes, while his mother seemed to be trading some stern words with Jeaneane, who kept pointing for them to leave. Grabbing her son's hand, the woman marched angrily back to her Volvo. Jeaneane, shaking her head, returned to the store.

I wanted to know what had happened. Perhaps the boy had broken something? But how can one operate a toy store without the implicit understanding that some of the merchandise will inevitably be damaged? In fact, I had heard that toy stores factored in a certain percentage of broken toys into their pricing structure. Maybe the mother had been caught trying to shoplift something. Her overcoat had seemed particularly bulky. Shoplifting has never been much of a problem at Halstein's, as our customers would feel far too guilty stealing from a business that has so clearly taken their well-being to heart. Yes, it must have been a shoplifting incident. I felt sorry that Miramack had to get off on the wrong foot like this on their first day of business.

Then a dad with two little girls entered the store. Barely two minutes later they were back out on the sidewalk, one girl in tears, the other wearing an expression of intense concern. Their father gestured boldly and I could hear that he was shouting but couldn't hear what was being said.

Perhaps the reason why I didn't intervene at this point was because my mind was simply not capable of concluding that Jeaneane didn't want these customers' business. There must have been some other factor as to why two customers in a row had been shown the door. I've had to deal with disruptive intruders before and have on occasion had to threaten to call the police. When an intoxicated or mentally unstable person disrupts the calm of the store, there is an opportunity for the proprietor to form a deeper bond with his legitimate customers. By taking the situation firmly in hand and demanding that the offending person leave, you show your patrons that you are concerned for their safety in a pleasant shopping environment. They really appreciate you for it. On a couple occasions where I have had to deal with unruly visitors, my customers have literally applauded me.

But I found it unbelievable that these families visiting Mira-mack had offended Jeaneane to such a degree that they would be asked to leave. After seeing three adolescent boys sulking out of the store, I decided I would use the welcome basket as a pretense for my investigation.

I found the store very attractively laid out, with some chil-dren's music playing, and a toy monkey riding a bicycle on a wire stretched from wall to wall overhead. Jeaneane sat behind her cash register reading a romance novel and eating a scone.

"First day of business, eh?" I said.

"What do you want?"

"Just stopping by to drop off this welcome basket. There are some soaps and fragrances and a few other goodies, all courtesy of Halstein's. To welcome you to the neighborhood."

"You can go ahead and put it on the table next to the rubber insects."

I did as I was directed and looked at some dolls lined up in their plastic-encased boxes.

"Nuh-uh," Jeaneane said. "Don't touch."

"Pardon?"

"You heard me. Don't touch the merchandise."

"Oh."

Jeaneane sighed. "I can tell I will be rattling off this same speech for the rest of my goddamn life. Look. We're a toy whole-saler, not a regular toy store. We only sell to buyers from toy stores, not the general public. We've got a warehouse out by the shipyard where we keep our stock. This is just a sampling of what we have. You come in here, you see something you like, you give us a P.O. and we ship it in minimum quantities of one pallet. That's how it works. So quit wasting my time and let me get back to my lunch and this trash I'm reading."

I was speechless. I must have walked back to the drugstore, but I can't remember crossing the street or anything that happened for half an hour. Such a store was inconceivable to me, an unbelievably cruel joke. That they would put their wares on such attractive display, hang an "Open" sign on their door, and entice children with a train set seemed like the retail equivalent of a Venus flytrap. And yet I could not fault their business model. Surely there needed to be places such as these, where professional buyers got to see the wares before they ordered them in bulk. I, for one, frequently visited such a wholesaler of over-the-counter remedies, but their offices were in a nondescript concrete building, not an attractive storefront. It killed me to watch kids get ejected from the premises time after time, and I had to explain Miramack's confusing scheme to many of my own customers who were understandably bewildered that they had been so rudely told to scram.

I kept my distance from Jeaneane, glancing up occasionally to see what she was doing across the street. I liked to think that she had enjoyed the basket, but she neglected to send a thank-you card. It may have been my imagination, but I believe her hair appeared to have a little more body, more bounce. She seemed to have no interest in my business at all, and I must admit that hurt a little bit. We coexisted for a month or so like this as summer slowly turned gray. I pulled back on the orders for sunscreen and weight loss supplements and started thinking about Halloween. It's my favorite time of year at the store, with all the kids and their parents coming in to try on costumes. Halloween gave me just the reason I needed to approach Jeaneane anew.

She barely looked up when I entered her store again. "I thought I told you we don't serve the general public," she mumbled.

"I'm not the general public. I am a small business owner and I am interested in purchasing toys for Halloween."

"You?" she said, her voice softening. "Your little store?"

"Are you telling me you only sell to places like Toys 'R' Us?"

"No, absolutely not. I'd be happy to show you some of the merchandise we're featuring for Halloween."

Jeaneane directed my attention to a bin full of rubber bats and spiders on elastic strings. There were glowing skull-headed flashlights, jack-o-lantern kits, and latex flesh wounds. Sure, everything was plastic and manufactured in Hong Kong, but it all appeared a cut above what my regular suppliers offered. I settled on a perennial classic—vampire fangs.

"You know you have to buy these by the pallet, right?" Jeaneane said.

"Absolutely. How many are in a pallet?"

"Six thousand. At ten cents a pair wholesale, that's $600. A steal. You can sell these puppies for fifty cents a pair, easy."

Six hundred dollars was about what I spent a week on cosmetics, cold remedies, and vitamins combined, but my sense of curiosity got the better of me. Jeaneane seemed to lighten up somewhat during the transaction, like my signing a purchase order moved something inside her. Then I made the mistake of telling her how great her hair looked, which I meant only as a subtle reminder that I had given her some premium quality shampoos.

"Are you hitting on me? Cause that can stop right now, Mister."

"Not at all! I simply—I just thought since I gave you those shampoos and—"

"Oh, the basket thing. I have no idea where that went. Sure."

"So anyway, feel free to come across the street sometime. We've got a special on panty hose right now."

"Do I look like the type of woman who wears panty hose?"

My blood pressure was up, which I later confirmed on Halstein's coin-op machine. For the first time in years I felt as though I had to fight for a customer. If I could have convinced Jeaneane to come to the store and buy just a book of stamps, I would have considered that a victory.

"Let me guess. You've worn panty hose in the past but felt them to be too constricting. You might try some graduated compression hosiery designed to accelerate movement of blood to the heart, which increases circulation and comfort," I said.

"I don't wear panty hose because they make me look like a slut."

"Well!"

"Your fangs should arrive by the end of the week."

True to her promise, the pallet of vampire fangs was obscuring my door when I opened on Friday morning. I sliced through the shrink wrap with a box cutter and stacked the individual cartons in a pyramid taller than me by the window.

"Whoa! That's a lotta fangs!" one of my regulars, Constance Grossman, said, dropping a package of Depends on the counter. "Somebody must have placed a mistaken order around here!"

"It's that time of year again, Mrs. Grossman. When all the goblins come out. Halstein's is your one-stop shop for all of your All Hallow's Eve essentials."

"I don't celebrate Halloween! These fangs are freaking me out!"

I carried Mrs. Grossman's purchases out to her car for her and when I returned there were two boys hitting each other with Wiffle ball bats in aisle three. I yelled at them perhaps more harshly than I should have. No two ways about it, I was having a bad customer service day.

When I was closing up that night, Jeaneane was sweeping the sidewalk in front of the store. I don't know who she was trying to impress. She stopped sweeping to call out, "Hey Bud, how are those fangs moving for you?"

"Just great!" I yelled back, though in truth I had sold two pairs. Only 5,998 to go.

"Too bad we don't have a returns policy!" Jeaneane laughed, and I had to restrain myself from giving her a rude gesture.

The next day I lowered the price of the fangs from fifty cents to twenty-five. I sold about ten pairs. My customers had simply not succumbed to Halloween fever yet. I watched a group of men and women in nice suits enter Miramack and emerge an hour later all smiles, with Jeaneane shaking their hands and even giving a couple of them hugs. Corporate types. Watching her bask in what was undoubtedly a lucrative transaction steamed me.

"So what's with all the fangs, Bud?" It was one of my longest-standing customers, Mr. Carlos DeLeon, who had shuffled in to purchase some diabetic candy and arthritis cream.

"What about them, Carlos? Don't you know Halloween is just around the corner? Why wouldn't we stock up on fangs this time of year?"

Mr. DeLeon looked taken aback. "Geez, Bud. I was just asking."

"Here, take a couple pairs. On the house. You look like a guy who could use some fangs."

"But they'll interfere with my dentures."

"Well don't you have any grandchildren?" I said.

"Why do you have to bring up that awful subject?" Mr. DeLeon said woefully. Right. His three grandchildren had all died in a boat fire the year before. I should have remembered.

"Look, just take the damn fangs."

Mr. DeLeon brusquely grabbed his bag and said, "You just lost yourself a customer, Bud. I hope you're happy."

I checked my blood pressure again. Through the roof. When I returned to the front of the store I heard the crash of shattering glass and a peeling-out car. Across the street the display window of Miramack's was shattered.

I found Jeaneane in her store clutching a brick in one bloody hand and a note in the other.

"Fucking kids. Look what they did."

The note read in crayon, "*Why dont you be a REAL toy store dooshbag???*"

"Your hand," I said. "Let me see."

She dropped the brick and her fingers pulled away from her palm like petals on a blooming flower. I carefully extracted a thin shard of glass from where the pistil would have been.

"I guess I panicked and grabbed some glass when I picked up the brick," she said, queasy.

"Come to my store. I'll fix you up." I led Jeaneane across the street by the wrist, elevating her hand. In the store I donned latex gloves and cleaned the wound with antiseptic, then dressed it in gauze. As I worked, I watched Jeaneane's eyes take in the place.

"Where are your other employees?" Jeaneane said.

"Right now, see, we're conserving costs by just staffing, well, me."

"And your stock. Jesus, some of this crap looks ten years old."

I smiled, took her hand, and gently applied pressure.

Jeaneane drew her hand away. "That's enough," she said, and without saying thank you she returned to her store to pick shards of glass from the trestle of the train set. Later, she duct-taped a garbage bag over the hole in her window. It billowed convex then concave based on the air pressure whenever the door opened or closed. Where once a professional-quality display of an alpine village and Lionel trains had beckoned passers-by, there was now just a rippling membrane of blackness. I assumed Jeaneane would contact her landlord to have a new pane installed, but several days passed and the garbage bag remained, a depressing reminder of some thoughtless boys' disrespect for small business owners' property.

While Halstein's has never had the staff or volume of business to justify remaining open 24/7, there have been occasions that I have kept the store open an hour or two past our posted hours.

It's advantageous for the business that my apartment is in the same building, up a flight of stairs in the back. Occasionally, during a commercial break or after I have cleaned the dishes, I come back down to the store when the lights are out and roam the aisles. Sometimes I take a basket from the rack up front and meander through the place as if I were a customer, holding bottles of tea tree oil shampoo up to the moonlight, frowning as if I can't decide whether it's worth the price. I will admit, too, that sometimes after my nightly bath I have returned to the store in my bathrobe. And I would not be honest if I didn't divulge the enjoyment I receive under cover of darkness, communing with the store in the nude. Nudity is nothing to be ashamed of. As a youth I spent many summers with my family at naturist colonies along the Oregon and Washington coasts. There we collected huckleberries and indulged in games of capture the flag clothing-free, and I attribute my positive attitude about the myriad ways the human body can exhibit beauty to these formative experiences. It pleases me a great deal to visit the aisles of Halstein's, basket a-brim with toe fungus medications and emery boards, wearing nothing but a shower cap.

A few weeks after the unfortunate incident of vandalism at Miramack's, on a night of terribly stormy weather, I found myself unable to sleep. I considered trying one of the new homeopathic insomnia remedies I had begun to carry, but decided instead to indulge myself and pretend I was a shopper while free of the strictures of garments. I put on my slippers and descended the stairs to the dark store. Products lined shelves like the setting of a magical cartoon, positively thrilling me with dormant revenue potential. I fetched a basket and headed for the deodorants and antiperspirants, where I selected a three-pack of Dove Silk Protection Anti-Perspirant/Deodorant for sensitive skin. Near enough to the front that I could see the street, I noticed that the storm had torn the garbage bag from Miramack's window. With the rain coming down hard, I feared that the toys within would get wet. Should I have gone upstairs and gotten dressed before I headed across the street to repair the window? It was two-fifty in the morning, and all the neighborhood bars had emptied their patrons, so I knew I wouldn't run into anyone if I simply jogged the ten paces to Miramack's and quickly assessed the situation. And perhaps it was the spirit of naturism, the sheer delight that comes from dancing nude in the rain, that clouded my judgment in this instance. I opened the door and found myself on the street, clothing optional, with a basket of toiletries under my arm.

Not only had the storm torn the garbage bag from the window, it appeared to have blown the door open as well. I nudged the ajar door open and carefully stepped inside. Immediately I was blinded by a bright light.

Someone rattled a spray paint can. "Holy *fuck*? Check it out, Horace, it's some fucking perv."

They struck me in the face with something metal, a toy truck, maybe. I fell to the floor, spitting blood. Five, six, a dozen blows, I lost track of how many times they hit me. They spoke of getting away with a case of Hot Wheels cars, and in a moment of bloody-faced blindness I understood that the stormy weather had nothing to do with the garbage bag being torn down. One of them stomped on my hand with his boot. I blacked out.

I came to the next morning and couldn't move. The storm had passed. Freight trucks beeped their backup alarms from distant warehouses. I opened my one good eye and saw one of my teeth in a pool of dried blood beside a plush Curious George toy and a packet of Listerine Fresh Burst Oral Care Strips. The door banged open.

"Jesus Christ! What happened?"

"Jeaneane?" I said. She rolled me onto my back. My voice came out funny. "Those kids again. I think the same ones who threw the brick. I came over. They took some Hot Wheels. . . . "

"Oh my God, and they took your clothes, too? You poor man." She helped me into a plush, elephant-shaped chair. "Sit tight, I'll get you some stuff from your store."

With my one nonswollen eye, I read the rude messages that had been spray painted on the walls of the store. A few minutes later Jeaneane returned with some bandages and antiseptic. As she tended to my abrasions she told me that the vandals who had hit her store had apparently hit mine as well. They had smashed glass cases and shattered the collectible figurines within. The aisles were strewn with fangs and prophylactics, the shelves denuded of candy and over-the-counter cough medicine.

I shivered as Jeaneane recounted the scene of devastation. She covered me with her fleece jacket, and I smelled the calendula-scented conditioner I had included in her welcome basket, clinging faintly to the collar.

Contaminant

My friends told me they'd pick me up around midnight but they didn't tell me I'd have to share the back seat with a corpse. Mitch, Charlie, and Avi all sat in the front, like those characters in *Saturday Night Fever,* looking like it was no biggie. The back seat was clearly more appropriate for two of them, but nobody wanted to sit next to the dead guy. It was raining and I was soaked to the point of not wanting to deal with their bull-shit. Somebody had to sit next to the corpse, and it was going to be me.

Mitch's car was some big old Pontiac or some other piece-of-shit car. The thing had three emblems from three different makes bolted to various parts of the exterior. The car used to be the tear-it-down/build-it-back-up vehicle the high school auto shop used before funding got tight and they eliminated all vocational tech. Mitch bought it for cheap and pretended like it was the best thing that ever rolled out of Detroit.

"If he drips or something on the leatherette, could you like use a towel to wipe it up?" Mitch said, his unibrow framed in the rear-view There was a pile of Motel 6 hand towels in the back seat next to the dead guy.

"Sorry, Mitch. It's not my job to clean dead guy residues off your back seat," I said.

Avi snorted and said something I couldn't hear to Charlie, who did his annoying giggle.

"Give me some slack," Mitch said, "he needed a ride."

"To where? The plant? Is he joining our carpool?"

Mitch cleared his throat. "Yeah, actually. It's his first day."

"Well if he's going to ride with us, we're going to have to rotate back seat duty, 'cause I'm not going to be the one stuck here every night with the towelettes worrying about your upholstery."

We rode in silence a while. That's not quite right. We rode listening to the talk radio station the three of them insisted on listening to. Tonight's topic was about whether most chicks have rape fantasies. About 75 percent of the callers seemed to be saying *yes, definitely,* which was pretty much the breakdown of opinion among those of us in the car who were not dead. I was the odd man out as always, purposely stuck back here with a decomposing newbie. I knew my friends hated me, mildly, for getting a promotion to the lab. We had always talked trash about the management, but since my promotion they'd been like, "Ooh, better not shit talk Peter around Doug here. He's all cozy with the higher-ups now." If only I hadn't had my license revoked I would have driven myself to work rather than relying on my stupid friends.

"So does the dead guy have a name?" I said.

"Yeah, my name's Clarence," the dead guy sighed, his words fogging the passenger side window. It was then that I noticed that the dead guy was black.

Avi snorted, Charlie giggled, and Mitch extended his arm out the window to give the bird to a guy who'd just cut him off. I was grateful when we pulled into the parking lot of the plant. I often marveled at how incredible it looked at night, its plumes and chutes and vats lit up like some kind of vast science fiction scenario. You could drive around for hours in this part of the country and never see anything taller than the tallest man who ever lived. Then, wow, in your headlights loomed a monument to human ingenuity such as this, our place of employment.

Avi and Mitch helped Clarence out of the car. Being his first day, he was going to have to get set up with Human Resources. I watched him shuffle stiffly across the parking lot and knew he wasn't going to last long. You needed to be quick on your feet at Trans World Vegetable, you needed to go double speed if there was a breakdown in the line. I wasn't going to have to worry about him being part of our company for long.

Inside, I put on the jumpsuit and protective face mask that identify me as Lab Tech Liaison. Here's how my job works—every pallet of peas that rolls down the line has to be tested for pesticide, disease, and fuel contamination. When the trucks come in and dump their loads, the raw peas go through a wash and are then frozen and deposited in a series of vats. The vats are located above our heads and have filtration systems that release the peas through a freezing chamber, after which they drop through a chute that extends over a particular portion of the conveyor belt. Thick cardboard boxes about the size of washing machines roll down the line and stop beneath the chute. The chute is equipped with a little door that can be opened and closed by whoever's manning that station. Between boxes, the door is shut, but as soon as a box is in position, the door is opened and a waterfall of frozen peas comes roaring out of the chute. During the box-filling process a guy known as a sampler takes a scoop of peas and puts it in one of those canisters like they use at the drive-up teller at the bank. This canister is put into a pneumatic tube that leads to the lab. I open the canister, distribute the peas to the personnel who perform the tests, and dump the peas into the waste. If I don't say anything, the peas keep rolling along. But if any tests come up positive, holy shit. In that case I hit the red button that shuts down the whole joint. I have to be able to distribute the peas quickly, because the door to the frozen pea chute can be closed for a maximum of two and a half minutes before the frozen peas are compacted into what is known as a pea clog. This has happened a few times at the plant, but never on my shift.

I can view the floor from behind a Plexiglas window. The part of the plant where I do my tests is responsible for the processing of peas for large food companies. Our peas end up in baby food and bags of premixed vegetable medleys. From my seat I can see my friends, who occasionally flip me off or grab their crotches when they know I'm watching.

That night I sat beside Thuy, who spoke very little English. I liked her, if only because I could rely on her to laugh at my jokes when no one else would. She'd done this kind of work in Korea, apparently. A pea between her white gloved fingers was an enigma to be unraveled. When I arrived I relieved Gary of his post. He was the kind of guy who had a Jesus fish eating a Darwin fish on the back of his Ford F-250. Even though Gary and I shared the same language, we didn't share the same sense of humor. Who knew what god Thuy worshipped or what she drove. I didn't care. I just appreciated someone who reacted audibly whenever I recited one of the approximately five hundred knock-knock jokes I have committed to memory.

I could see Clarence getting oriented at the box station. The forewoman, Theresa, appearing a little grossed-out by the whole ordeal, nonetheless showed Clarence how to quickly assemble a box, secure it with a steel band, and insert a blue plastic liner. These boxes were then loaded onto pallets, which were in turn loaded onto the conveyor belt. The boxes had been used before, so any distinguishing markings had to be covered up with brown tempera paint. All this had to be accomplished in about five minutes per box. If you got fast and created a surplus of boxes all waiting to be loaded onto the conveyor, you could chill a little bit, take a smoke break or get something from one of the snack machines.

At first Clarence seemed confused by various stages of the box-making process. What happens to your brain when you die, anyway? Does it decompose slower, encased in bone and not exposed to the elements? A couple times the forewoman had to come over and build a couple boxes herself, but it did seem

Clarence was giving it his best try. The first night is always rough for a new guy getting accustomed to the hectic pace of a plant.

The C Shift meal break happened at 4 A.M. sharp. I know this might sound ethnically not-nice of me, but I was glad Thuy had a different meal break than me, because she ate that fishy Vietnamese or whatever food it was that overpowered the break room smell-wise.

"Knock knock," I said.

"Who there?" Thuy said.

"Saul."

"Saul who?"

"Saul good to me, I'm gonna go get me some lunch!"

When I got to the break room, Avi, Mitch, and Charlie were all sitting at a table with Clarence, who had a seat open beside him. So I got my lunch from the C Shift fridge and sat at a different table with Henry, the forklift operator who, rumor had it, had once, in a single setting, ingested enough magic mushrooms to get our whole county high. You couldn't tell by looking at him. He wore the same flannel shirt and Peterbilt hat to work every day. Apparently he had some kind of girlfriend with a kid by another guy. Occasionally, his paranoid literature would show up on the floor of the men's john—zines and printed-out Web pages detailing more than your run-of-the-mill conspiracies. The JFK assassination was like vanilla ice cream to Henry. The Illuminati, the Freemasons, just fronts for organizations way more badass. He seemed to accept the underlying corruption of the ways of men as par for the course. His theories occupied him, and we were amused by his conviction that a half dozen people in a hollowed-out mountain in West Virginia controlled the world's coffee supply.

Henry was eating a tuna sandwich, a bag of Fritos, and some carrot sticks with a Mountain Dew, a lunch that struck me, oddly, as utterly psychotic.

"You like Air Supply, right?" Henry said.

"Eighties band? Power ballads?" I said.

"Yeah."

"They were okay I guess."

"I've got a story for you then," Henry said, chewing his sandwich, "that is, if you're into either Air Supply or retarded people."

I was into neither, but I still wanted to hear Henry's story. I told him I was very interested in both.

Henry sighed, like he'd told this story many times before and was annoyed at having to tell it again. "So I got new neighbors at the duplex. They're retarded in a for-real way. A man and a woman. They're married. When the man comes home from work his wife runs out onto the yard and they kiss a really long time. He told me his name is Roger-Roger, which I think is his nickname for regular Roger. The woman's name is Penelope. We've had some really involved conversations about when the recycling truck comes. I'm going out on a limb but I'm guessing you've never lived next door to someone who is retarded."

"Yeah."

"So, okay, the story. I hear this racket the other night, my wall is all vibrating. I go out to the yard in my pajamas and there's like this strobe light going *wong wong wong* from inside their place. I creep up to the window, through their flower bed. Roger is in there holding a microphone, serenading Penelope. He's singing her Air Supply songs on a new karaoke system it must have taken the guy months to save up for. Later, I find out that the karaoke machine plays *only* Air Supply songs. Like it came incomplete, with just the Air Supply cartridge. And I'm there laughing my ass off, which is okay, because he can't hear me or see me anyway."

Henry finished his sandwich and zoned out a while into his crumb-covered cellophane sandwich wrapper. Then he leaned forward and put his hand on my shoulder like a priest. I reminded myself that in the seventies guys used to drop seven hits of acid at once in order to be declared legally insane, and thus escape the draft. Henry opened his mouth as if to speak and seemed to be struggling to not cry.

"And then . . . then I looked at her face, man. It was so full of love. She was crying with joy. It was the most beautiful thing I have ever seen in my whole goddamn life."

Henry coughed and a tiny fleck of chewed-up bread landed on my forearm. I didn't know what to do while he composed himself so I just stared at my banana a while.

"So, you met the new guy yet?" I said finally, nodding my head toward the table where my friends sat.

"Met him? I fucking watched him die, man."

After that freaky conversation with Henry, I was ready to escape back into my work space. I never did find out what he'd meant when he said he had watched Clarence die, and I knew that if I pressed him on it he would yank me further down into his de-stroyed cerebellum. If I told one of my knock-knock jokes to Henry, he probably would spend ten minutes thinking about it and then break into tears.

There was the microbe-infested dirt where the peas grew, then a partition of Plexiglas separating me from the grease-smudged faces of my coworkers. Maybe they hated me because I'd escaped the crud and grime and stifling heat they had to work in. Maybe if I had been promoted to floor monitor or night supervisor my friends wouldn't have flipped me crap. The same sterilized envi-ronment that protected me from contaminants also gave their gripes about management a convenient target. That someone like me would be a friend to management was a joke. But because I was enclosed in a clean world inside a sterile jumpsuit, I was able to pass for somebody who was actually important. To rub it in, I suspected, they had gone and made a friend of a dead man.

Toward the end of my shift, I opened a canister and began pour-ing the peas out into their receptacles. Something tumbled out that looked like one of those bigger-sized Tootsie Rolls. I retrieved it from the receptacle and stared at it a couple seconds. It was a human thumb. The skin was eaten away in places, revealing gray muscles underneath. The nail was half off, stuck to the flesh with a substance that looked like rubber cement. The top of the finger was pigmented dark black, fading to a beige color on the under-side. There were only two black people who worked this shift, and the thumbnail sure as hell didn't have little sailboats and palm trees painted on it, so I knew the finger didn't belong to Marlene.

"Injury on the line!" I yelled, smacking the red alarm button. The lights and alarms ripped through the plant like Christmas on crack. There were wheezing sounds of machines and exhaling hydraulics as the line shut down station by station. Thuy put the thumb in a Ziploc and placed it in the refrigerated safe designed to isolate contaminants. On the other side of the Plexiglas the crew was either running around frantically or standing ineffectually in place. Even though the line was down and no more peas were being loaded at input, I knew there were several tons of frozen peas above our heads that needed to get in boxes or else we'd have one hell of a pea clog to contend with. Whoever was responsible for the chute had hightailed it out of there, so a steady torrent of peas had filled a box and was overflowing onto the floor. One of the supervisors ran by, slipped on frozen product, and banged his head on the floor in what promised to be a pretty nasty OSHA claim.

I ripped off my mask and barreled through the doors. At that moment I knew what it must have felt like to be Bruce Springsteen.

"Davis, climb back up there and close the goddamn chute! Rasmussen, Sanchez, grab a couple brooms and clear the product from the walkway! Barrett, don't just stand there, take Gus to the break room and call him an ambulance! Ortiz, Jackson, Hellman, I'm going to need your help redirecting the line!"

With a fire axe in hand I climbed up to the edge of the belt, careful to avoid stepping on any of its lubricated wheels. One of these pallets was going to have to move and there was no way, with a ton of peas on top if it, that brute strength was going to make it happen. I slammed the axe into the side of the box, slicing clean through the steel band. I murdered that thing. Peas spilled out through the conveyor onto the floor. Soon we were able to get the pallet out of the way, close the trap, and disconnect the stanchion joints. We had a minute by my guess. We swung this section of the line over so it hung out into space and had Henry bring over the fork lift so he could manually grab each pallet and drive it over to an open part of the floor. After about twenty boxes the vat over our heads ran dry. My quick thinking ended up saving us a costly maintenance procedure, not to mention several tons of peas. By the time the owner of the plant showed up, tipsy at 10 A.M., the floor was clear, the line was reconnected, and operations were running at capacity again. Human Resources sent Clarence packing.

I was promoted to Assistant Manager of Plant Operations. Production has increased by a respectable 2.3 percent since I suggested a number of reforms. The plant actually cranks out more peas per hour now without an increase in line speed, meaning we produce greater volumes with the same amount of human labor. Sometimes managers from other Trans World plants come out to visit and I show them the simple things you can do to cut out redundancies and reduce downtime. Trans World has flown me out to a couple under-producing plants, even paid for my meals and hotel, to turn things around.

My friends still work graveyard, and sometimes I see them on weekends, at barbecues or softball games. I've been making friends with some of the folks in the front office. They're just people with tons of shit to do like any of us. I told Avi he could use my parking space since we work different shifts. He says his car would look conspicuous next to the Lexuses, but I know he turned down my offer out of respect.

So I guess I could leave it there and come out smelling like a champion, but there's a postscript here I'd be dishonest to leave out. A couple nights after the disconnected thumb incident I decided to walk home instead of getting a ride with Avi. The sun is usually coming up by the time I finish my shift, and this particular morning the refineries must have been burning something awful because the sky was gorgeous. Like the bloody wound from the chemical burn poster in the break room stretched gloriously across the horizon. I walked through town, passing gas stations and subdivisions, a whole world of people just getting up and starting their day as I was finishing mine. I watched a woman forget that she had left her coffee tumbler on top of her minivan then pull out of her driveway, screaming at her kids. A cop nodded at me from behind the windshield of his cruiser. It felt pretty great to be out here like this, even though I looked and smelled like shit. I recognized Henry's pickup truck with the Krokus and Dokken bumper stickers and remembered about the Air Supply–singing retards. I found the duplex in question and snuck around back to the sliding door to the kitchen. There were cookie jars and Jell-O molds in there, a coffee pot with brown rings marking different layers of evaporation. I wanted to see something beautiful. I wanted to go inside, so I did.

Civilization

When I turned eighteen I was among the kids who received notice that it was time to make some sacrifices and fulfill our duties as Americans. My family had been receiving letters from the government since we'd registered as a nuclear unit. We had learned to discard the notes asking us to watch certain shows, skim the flyers with health and hygiene tips, and set aside the forms having to do with money or the variety of multiple-choice quizzes that gauge our happiness. People living in less regulated times and places would probably raise their freedom-loving eyebrows at the idea of the government telling everybody what to do. But this era has its bennies, as anyone like my grandparents, who straddled the ages, can confirm.

"Those were some hella shitty times," my grandfather says from his vibrating Barcalounger at The Home.

"Fer sure," says my grandmother.

I'm a profiled procrastinator, and knew I had two months before I had to report to my Duty Manager to perform the terms of my duty. I tried to pretend that the remainder of my senior year was unburdened by what I had been asked to do. I imagined that the texture of my daily existence—hanging out with friends, eating bad-for-me food, petting heavy with a girl in the back seat of my dad's Buick—was the template from which everyone's life took cues. Yeah, but I had this "thing" hanging over me, this immense, democratic responsibility. I tried to ignore my looming duty by pouring software and Coca-Cola Classic Classic ("The cocaine is back!!!") into my head. But no matter which distraction technique I attempted, I could not escape the malformed, rotting mass of fear sitting on my chest every time I remembered that the USA had asked me to murder my parents.

Because I liked them well enough. They'd given me some great presents over the years, made me some fine meals. And while I didn't feel ready to perform what was expected of me, they nonetheless provided the same unwavering support they always had, like when I wrestled freestyle a whole season and never won a single match.

My dad, short, wearing a tie by way of description, offered me a beer and made some noises about personal responsibility. My mom, who unlike my dad had been called to duty back in the day, said it was really a quick procedure, that I'd have my choice of instruments, and that she'd try not to make too much noise. Then we sat down as a family to watch the Homeless People Channel, and seeing those guys pushing their shopping carts around really made me feel like I had a lot of resources—natural and otherwise—to be thankful for.

Civilization

My friends, of which none had yet received duty papers, intensified my nervousness with stories of kids who'd only halfkilled their folks, who'd had to chase them down stairwells, hunt them in cornfields, even deal with their moms and dads fighting back. (Both my parents had assured me they wouldn't struggle.) Or the stories about brothers and sisters of duty-bound kids who'd strangled their siblings in the night to spare their folks. Luckily I was an only child, and one of the benefits of performing my duty was a paid-in-full scholarship to the college or university of my choice. I wasn't going to blow it like the stupid kids who signed up for Harvard and dropped out during the first semester, thereby losing their free ride. I already had my eye on a little East Coast college no one had ever heard of that had a fantastic Egyptology program. Call me weird, but I've always had a thing for mummies and pyramids.

At school, my teachers let me slack that semester, aware of the enormous responsibility weighing so very hippo-like on my formative young mind. I openly smoked the cheeb in the back of class, and they didn't even make me drop Western Civ and take Rehab or Home Ec instead. You could get away with shit like that at my high school when you were assigned the task of preserving American democracy.

After school one day I went to pick out caskets with my folks, and even though I would be tapping into my own grieving stipend to foot the bill, I let them choose any style they wanted.

"Are you positive? We really shouldn't spend so much," my mom said. I could tell she had her eye on the "Freedom Through

Strength" model, the curly maple one with the engraving of an American eagle clutching a bouquet of nuclear missiles in one talon and an Osama bin Laden head in the other. My dad picked the classic American flag model that plays the song of your choice when opened and "Taps" when closed, even though he was never in the service. My dad told the casket coordinator that he wanted it to play the patriotic hit song written by the software band Mugwump 2.0. While I usually clashed with my dad over our music tastes, that song, "Lightning Will Strike Our Enemies (And I'm Feelin' Good About It)," had been a real cross-generational hit and had even kicked the hypothetical Francis Scott Key's ass in the reality show "National Anthem Smackdown."

Afterward, we went out to dinner at this Italian-themed restaurant called Il Italiano and talked about my future plans, but really the only thing in my head was a loop of the following words: gun, knife, poison, blunt instrument, gun, knife, poison, blunt instrument. On top of that—Kee-*rist!*—I still hadn't taken the frickin' SATs. Even though they were a formality at this point, I still had promised my parents to shoot for at least an 1100. To feel better, I kept reminding myself they'd be dead when I got the results in the mail.

Our waitress, Pam, came by with the salad and breadsticks. "Who wants pepper?" she said, bearing her mill. "Just tell me when." None of us were stepping up to the responsibility of being the pepper when-sayer, so Pam kept cranking over the mound of iceberg, olives, and pepperoncinis. "Whoa. You folks must-a really like-a the peppa!"

"Enough," my dad said, raising his hand. For a second I allowed myself to believe he was referring to this me-killing-them business.

"Fantastico," Pam said. "We have two specials tonight, a pesto radiatore with grilled salmon fillet and a raquetella with creamy gorgonzola sauce and peas. Now, I don't expect you to know all these fancy Italian pasta names, so let me tell you that raquetella are little tennis racquet shapes. The peas are supposed to be like the tennis balls. Can I get you started with some artichoke spinach dip or ranch cheesy bread?"

"I don't care what we have," I said.

My dad cleared his throat. "Our son has been called upon to perform his duty for this great land of ours."

"Oh shit," I said, knowing what happened in these kinds of places when they learned you'd been served duty papers. And sure enough, three minutes later the entire wait staff of fifteen was crowded around our table clapping rhythmically and singing one of those dippy patriotic songs from the employee manual.

"This is bullshit!" I shouted. "I don't want to kill you! I love you!"

"*Please*," my mom said through lips stretched to the point of losing blood, "we're in a *restaurant*."

My father nodded to the restrooms and said, "Go take a chill pill, Craig, and come back when you're ready to have a mature discussion about performing your duty."

As I tearfully left the table I heard my father nervously chuckling, telling the assembled wait staff that it was just some to-be-expected performance anxiety on my part. I was starting to see

how seriously fucked my situation really was. My parents would
never see things my way, because in their mind I was still just a
kid. And if I didn't go through with the killings, the government
would tax my family into poverty and I wouldn't get a chance to
study Egyptology at the college of my choice.

The Il Italiano men's room had one of those urinals that played
"Flight of the Valkyries" when you peed into it, which I hated.
Eating at Il Italiano over the years had conditioned me to race to
the bathroom during one of my favorite scenes in that classic
movie *Apocalypse Now Redux II*.

I popped one of my chill pills from its foil wrapper and
washed it down with warm water from the sink. After I freshened
up I returned to the table, apologized, and had some on-the-
house house salad. My parents pretended my outburst never
happened.

My parents had a lot of things to take care of before they died,
and their final weeks were crammed with meetings with the title
company, insurance agents, accountants, lawyers. In between all
the meetings, though, they still managed to spend quality time
with me. One afternoon my mom was cool enough to suggest
that I skip fifth period and meet her for coffee. When I arrived at
the place, she was talking to two of her friends from the State
Lottery Commission, ladies who I suspected I could have gotten
in the sack had older chicks been my thing.

Catherine, the tall one whose nipples always showed through
her blouse and bra, ruffled my hair when I sat down at the minia-

ture table. "Gloria, take a look at this young man," Catherine said. "Just a couple three years ago he was playing army men in the conference room and now he's about to do the shit work of making America proud."

"Your mom and I were just talking about when we had to perform the duty," Gloria said. She was one of those cat lady types who is disappointed if visitors to her condo fail to comment on the zaniness of her Elvis shrine. "I must have bashed my pop over the head fifty times before the son of a bitch gave up the ghost."

"They gave you blunt instruments?" I said.

"Honey," Gloria said, "back in the day we didn't have no arsenic pills. We had to do things the hard way, isn't that right, Sally?"

My mom looked down and smiled, as if she was embarrassed about how she'd shot my maternal grandparents. I got the sense she considered her duty easy compared to Gloria, and didn't want to appear too smug about it.

"Yeah, mom, tell everyone how you offed Grandma and Grampa," I said.

"It's not worth telling."

"Oh sure it is," Gloria said. "Go on, Sally, your own son is old enough."

"It's not that interesting, really," my mom said. "They gave me a choice of a Mach II machine pistol, a .44 Magnum, or a .38 Special. Since I was a girl they made all the plastic hardware pink with flowers on it."

"Pathetic," Catherine said.

"My duty officer told me the best bet was the .38, but I wanted to really do some damage, you know, just to show off. So I chose the .44."

Chuckling, anticipating the punch line, Gloria said, "Come on, that's not all."

My mom sighed. "Okay, sure, I was nervous. And in those days let me just tell you, I know it's hard to believe, but I weighed 100 pounds in the rain. Don't give me that look; I'm serious! So unfortunately I blanked out on all those shooting classes I'd taken to prepare for this very special day, because I must have locked my elbows and the thing just kicked and knocked me flat on my rear end."

Catherine and Gloria howled, slapping the miniature table we were gathered around.

"So there I am, on my back, with a big bump on my head, and it turns out I missed my dad by a mile. My mom is cussing up a storm, my duty officer is leaning over me asking how many fingers he's holding up, it was just a mess. In the end I went with the machine pistol and that was that."

"Didn't you feel bad?" I said.

"Well, sure, for a little while. But they gave me the pill."

Gloria made a face. "I heard in the early days they didn't give kids the pill. I can't imagine. Whatever you do, Craig, *take the goddamn pill!*"

"What's the pill?" I said, worrying that I had missed mention of it in the brochure I'd been sent.

"The pill makes it all better," Catherine said. "It makes it impossible to feel like shit about what you just did. I feel funny saying this, but it's almost Orwellian."

"You're thinking of Huxley," Gloria said. "*Brave New World* was the one where they were always popping pills. Like that part when they all go to Spring Break and party with the Beatles."

I felt as though I had stumbled into some foreign and primal feminine ritual. As the women continued to talk, their voices faded away like they sometimes do on TV, when they want to indicate a character has just been slipped something in a drink.

Poison, shotgun, length of chain.

They abducted my parents while I slept, allowing them time to gather some personal effects and leave me a note on a Post-It on the kitchen island. "Good luck, Craig! Don't let your nerves get to you!" read my father's blocky handwriting. I would have a day to contemplate my upcoming actions. I spent it like many teens who've been selected for duty, moping around the house, trying to chill out to the Sleeping Babies channel. My friends called to razz me because I'd been mentioned on the news and the anchorman had hilariously bungled the pronunciation of my last name. I attempted to will into being a series of events that would save my parents and me, a string of happenstance and luck that spiraled outward into a self-generating parallel reality. In my daydream my parents were rescued from their confinement by some kind of paramilitary freedom fighter guys that in this reality only existed as contestants on game shows. I left my house through the back door, jogged across the yard, climbed over the fence and ran through the wheat field abutting our property, and this wheat field, instead of ending at Parkway Road with the Deli Mart that has the porno mags, extended uninterrupted across this grand continent, and while I ran, naked now in my imagination, a farmer on a tractor would occasionally tip his hat and call out, "Way to go, son! You keep on a-runnin'!"

And it was maybe indicative of my own maturing process that I quickly pressed Pause on this fantasy and declared it stupid and infantile in my head.

The duty officer who arrived at my house in her mid-sized sedan looked not much older than me. Her name was Tisha. She smacked her gum and wore a red, white, and blue tracksuit.

"All right," Tisha said, "Looks like we're ready. Are you totally psyched? I went through the procedure myself and can't tell you how much it has positively changed my life. Don't worry, you're going to do fine. I met your parents this morning at the center and can tell you they're really swell folks, they want you to do a good job. They'll be so proud of you up to the moment they die."

As we pulled out of the driveway I declined Tisha's offer of Juicy Fruit.

"You read *1984*, right?" Tisha said, taking a free right. "Ha! I know you did, I reviewed your school transcripts. Well anyway, I tell people who are maybe a little nervous just to think of that one part where Winston Smith kicks down the door of his neighbors and catches them smoking crack. Then the part when he turns to the hidden camera and says, 'Time to unleash a lil' whoop-ass, what do you say, Big Bro?' and then he smokes those dirty hippies with his Glock! I know, you're going: like what does this have to do with sending mom and pop to the boneyard. So what I'm saying is, you're going to have a real genuine American kind of moral authority real soon here, unleashing your own personal whoop-ass on your mom and dad for the sake of all our heterosexual liberties."

The mid-sized sedan took a couple sharp turns and we passed the historic district with the office parks and brick-and-mortar schools, then the stadiums and the focus group factories where people like my soon-to-be retired parents worked. And the flaming sun was a chariot racing across the sky and I thought how incredible it would have been to be an Egyptian engineer shepherding gigantic blocks of limestone across the desert. How a guy with that kind of mindset would not be capable of comprehending such things as terrorists who hate us for having a movie rating system that includes P for Penetration.

We got to the Duty Center, which used to be a post office. They even had a faded poster for commemorative Marilyn Monroe and James Dean stamps in one of the windows. When I couldn't or maybe wouldn't get out of the sedan, two beefier-style duty officers named Mike and Otto extracted me. Inside, they handcuffed me to a waiting room chair. There were three other kids sitting in the dusty semidarkness next to a table piled with old *Reader's Digests* with all the naughty parts censored with felt pen. We all looked nauseated and miserable, which struck me as ironic given that we were all recipients of free-ride scholarships. I read a little "Humor in Uniform" to pass the time. After a few minutes a door opened and a kid appeared with his designated duty officer. The kid was my age, with blood spattered on his seriously grinning face. It was the kind of grin that looks fused in place, a grin accompanied by laughter generating in the back of the throat. As soon as the girl sitting beside me saw him she put her head between her knees and puked into a receptacle one of the duty officers had thoughtfully provided.

One by one the kids ahead of me were called back by their own personal duty officers, and one by one they returned about twenty minutes later clutching their college admissions paperwork, weeping, shaking, or passed out in a wheelchair. I told myself I was just going to get it over with and keep thinking of the pyramids. Then my name was called and I followed Tisha, who now had a more serious demeanor, down a hall that seemed longer than the building we were in. At the end of the hall was a door that had been painted over many times, as if the room behind it had served many purposes over the years. Tisha opened the door onto a tiny, well-lit room where my parents sat back-to-back in fold-out metal chairs, arms bound behind them. My mom's makeup was smeared down her cheeks and my dad's hair was ruffled. On a nearby table sat a fillet knife, a meat cleaver, and some kind of oriental sword. Dammit. I'd been hoping I'd be one of those kids who lucked out and got a selection of poisons and a pair of syringes.

"You are about to perform an essential function of preserving American democracy for generations to come," Tisha said. "I'll be out here in the hall if you need me. Just holler."

Here we were, then, a family. My mom made a choking sound and her lips were quivering.

"Just get this over with, Craig," my dad said.

"I don't want to do this," I said.

"Do it!" my dad shouted, the same kind of shout he used when he was tired of reminding me to mow the lawn.

I approached the table and considered my weapons. "The fillet knife is the sharpest," my mom sobbed, "but the blade looks flimsy."

"If you want my honest opinion, I'd go with the sword," my dad said.

"It's too heavy and dull," my mom said.

"Craig can handle it. He'll just have to use both hands."

"I think this is Craig's decision."

"I'm not saying it isn't, honey. I do think, though, that the meat cleaver is out of the question."

I selected the fillet knife and stood in front of my mother, and my admiration for her having performed this duty twenty-odd years ago grew.

"Just do it," my mom whispered. I stabbed her in the chest. She gasped a deep, rattling breath. I took a step back and left the knife quivering, lodged between two ribs. She slowly looked down, her eyes ripped wide.

"Oh my god," I said.

"You're not done. . . . " my mom gasped.

"I can't!"

My mom scowled, blood sliding out the corners of her mouth. "Craig, you pussy, finish the job."

What followed I guess was some sort of blacked-out murderous rage. There was some missing footage and then I was sitting in a corner of the room, the three bloodied instruments lying on the floor, my folks slumped dead in their chairs.

After awhile Tisha leaned down and offered me the pill and a glass of water. The pill was stamped with a picture of the president's face with a cartoon word bubble containing the words, "Say No To Terror."

"It'll make it impossible for you to feel remorse for this later on," Tisha said. "Trust me. Taking the pill is the most important part of the process. Not taking it will turn the rest of your life into a nightmare."

Things turned out swell for me after fulfilling my duty, and I have to admit I'm a little embarrassed about how big a deal I made of it at the time. I write these recollections two years later in an encampment south of Cairo, where I am in charge of cleaning the equipment for a dig. The remains of a teeming city lie just beneath the shifting sands. The camels tonight are especially flatulent. An occasional fighter jet drags a contrail across the sky on its way to bomb countries that stubbornly refuse to let us help them achieve the American dream. I have watched a man lose his leg after falling off a train. I have smoked hashish and found myself in bars speaking to German textile plant owners trying to sell me their daughters. I have gazed upon the freaking Rosetta Stone. Digging through this barren landscape to uncover cities where real people once worked and raised families thrills me. I can't imagine going back to America. My life's true pleasures I have found in the remains of this lost, proud culture, in the solitude of their beautiful tombs.

Written by
Machines

It was autumn 1999 and Optimum Synergies was flush with venture capital. OS was this spin-off of a company called Optimum Optics, founded by a Microsoft exec who'd since quit the board to throw himself at a peer-to-peer model fated to implode in the wake of Napster. OS was a pup by startup standards, with give or take fifty employees occupying the third floor of an old office building in downtown Bellevue, Washington. Three weeks after they hired me as a tester in late '98, the three people who had interviewed me were gone, either seduced by other prospects or driven out by interdepartmental warfare with fuck-you money in hand. Having just received my certification, not yet appreciative of the ridiculous amplitude of my salary, I went to work as a member of the 15-head Quality Assurance team, beta testing some app of dubious value for Palm.

My paternal grandfather had operated a 200-acre berry farm that had since been sold to a company that converted the land into a seasonal agricultural attraction with a corn maze and display gardens. My dad owned the last standing independent hardware store in Issaquah, the town where I grew up. I completed the triptych as my family's representative of the information age. Grilling salmon one weekend in the backyard of the house he'd lived in for twenty-five years, my dad wanted to know what it was my company actually did.

"We've got our fingers in everything. We create internetworking solutions for mid-market Customer Relationship Management applications. We design, QA, and market wireless transfer apps in conjunction with Terabeam, these guys who use lasers to deliver packets within urban office building grids. We're working on a database query tool that'll function as a GUI off Miran cards to track call center volumes and productivity."

"I'm sure what you're doing is important to somebody," my dad said, opening the hood of the barbecue to check the pinkness of the salmon. Great satanic tendrils of smoke burned our eyes. I was confident I had fulfilled the single obligation he demanded of me as a son: I was making money. But I was doing it, he seemed to think, in a dubious manner, if my inadherence to any conventional dress code was a reliable measure. I didn't have to wring dollars from drywall screws like he had, or stoop to such humiliating marketing schemes as draping a banner across the front of his building proclaiming, *We declare war on Home Depot!* I wanted my father to be impressed with what I was doing, if only as revenge for all the shit he flipped at me for being too into computers as a kid. So I erected an unscalable barrier of lingo between us. It saddens me now. Feigning indifference to how much I was making, I rubbed his face in tech jargon, blowing the one opening he ever gave to me to convince him that my passions were deserving of his admiration.

A fork stabbed into a fish. Aunts, uncles, cousins beckoned. The clouds parted over the backyard, sending down golden sun shafts, like Sunday school depictions of angelic visitors. It was my job to organize the croquet. In the kitchen my mother assembled kabobs and sharpened her opinions on how her siblings should parent their children, as though she'd done such a superb job with me. The whole Western Washington side of my family was here, cajoling, dipping concave snack foods into processed dips, asking me to explain again how stock options worked. They thought I had all the answers.

I waded through the guts of our systems fourteen hours a day searching for bugs. Sloppier members of the QA team would simply fix the fucked-up lines that brought our systems to a standstill, but I took the time to optimize the code, condense fifty lines of PERL into a single, elegant subroutine. Years of stacking cans of spackle and sealant and primer label-side-out on shelves had conditioned me to tweak my work and leave my code in anal condition. I didn't pull shit like inserting little jokes into the scripts like some of my colleagues. My code was textbook beautiful.

For my efforts I was noticed and promoted to a special project that only a half dozen people in the company knew about, the mutant offspring of what had originally been a speech recognition app. Just five guys in a room, four of them still in their early twenties, banging on a trio of quad processors trying to bring something to life. Their names are unimportant, and I'm leery of litigation, so I'll refer to them by the nicknames derived from *Happy Days* that I secretly gave them. They had been working on an application that suggested words and phrases for passages of unintelligible spoken audio data. For instance, if I were to say, *The house I live in is blue*, rendering the word "house" unintelligible, the system analyzed the passage based on root-satellite syntactical hierarchies to determine that I had spoken the word "house" with 93 percent accuracy. It was the 7 percent that bothered Potsie, Ralph Malph, Chachi, and The Fonz. Sometimes the system produced ludicrous suggestions. Instead of inferring that I had meant to say the word "house," it would suggest "stomach." Nobody got why this was the case, particularly when the rest of the paragraph had nothing at all to do with digestion, internal organs, or food. Ralph Malph and Potsie had been butting their skulls against the system for a month trying to figure out where these interpolations were coming from. I did my thing and within a week the system was running at 95 percent accuracy. Still, though, those weird substitutions kept popping up.

Near the end of a 15-hour coding marathon, I came to several lines that I thought must have been a hallucination. It was some of the weirdest stuff I had ever seen, a crazy sequence of counterintuitive if-then statements that pinged a bootleg dictionary database cribbed from the OED. It appeared to be reading the dictionary and substituting words at random. That it was feeding from an exotic IP address was an instant tip-off that something wonky was going down. And I'd never seen such elegant and creative subroutines. This code hadn't sprung from the minds of Xbox-addicted geeks without girlfriends. This code belonged in the realm of Jimi Hendrix. This code was Michael Jordan hitting a three-pointer with a second on the clock to win the championship.

I confronted my colleagues with a couple pages of the stuff. "Who wrote this? Who would write something as seriously screwy as this?"

The conversation devolved into accusations and posturing. Finally The Fonz said, "Oh, man. I bet Wannamaker wrote it."

Right, Kevin Wannamaker. He'd been fired three months prior for surfing porn beyond a level our HR department would tolerate. Word was he'd parlayed his skills into policing online auction sites for libelous and fraudulent content. I'd seen the famous jpeg of him from the previous summer's company picnic, wearing an honest-to-God loincloth and Day-Glo war paint, hoisting a flaming lacrosse stick during some sort of joke athletic competition.

I had no ties to Kevin Wannamaker so I was tasked with tracking him down. It wasn't hard. I told him who I was over the phone and he laughed, coughed, and invited me to come over. He lived in a Belltown condo painted matte black, a pad crammed with eviscerated servers and sci-fi paperbacks, the foyer littered with hastily torn-open orange plastic delivery bags from Kozmo.com. Kevin, sick, thin, and bald, was wrapped in a blanket and moved languidly around a room lit only by computers.

On one of the monitors on the coffee table looped an animation of something unspeakably grotesque. He nudged a mouse with his bare toe and brought back the desktop, crowded with Excel file icons superimposed upon pornographic wallpaper.

"They told you I was canned for surfing porn well *fuck* them. You can look at the logs themselves and see my porn surfing wasn't nearly as elaborate as some of the other perverts who worked there. The real reason I was canned was because they wanted my system for themselves. I managed to extract my most important code before they got to it, the cocksuckers."

"Where were you going with it?" I said. "It seems incomplete."

"Of course it's incomplete. Didn't you catch the part about how I yanked all the best shit before I was even out the door? Do they know you've come to see me?"

I nodded.

"Screw it if they do. I'm giving myself three more weeks of this chemo shit and then I'm pulling a Cobain."

So his baldness wasn't intentional. And his milky, fluorescent face wasn't simply that way from hours of surfing. I told him I was sorry, the thing you're supposed to say to people dying of cancer.

"Fuck sorry. It's entirely avoidable. Living, breathing, drinking three hundred–plus chemicals that didn't exist before World War II, Jesus Christ. No surprises there. But man, heartless Optimum Synergies cutting a guy off his insurance, making him sell his Amazon stock to pay for chemo just for checking out bukkake clips on company time ha ha ha."

Kevin walked slowly into the kitchenette to find his bong. When he returned he fired up a bowl and sank into his plush couch. There was no place for me to sit so I continued to stand.

"I may die but my poetry system won't," he said.

"Poetry?"

"Yeah like Blake, like freakin' Byron, like Sylvia Plath. Didn't you do your fucking homework? Didn't they brief you? Didn't they provide you with my dossier?" Kevin launched a coughing fit I helped subdue with a glass of water. "Here, read some of this shit. Aloud," he said.

I picked up a stack of pages. *"Eclipse and smart card wrangling / Perfume bloody ripe oranges,"* I read.

"I think it might be a love poem," Kevin said.

"Looks like a random collection of words to me."

"What do you think poetry is? That's what I thought at first, too. But I kept reading and finding meanings in them. I don't understand 99 percent of this shit, but maybe that's because my human intelligence isn't as developed as that of the system."

"It's a random word generator. Spitting out gibberish."

"But see, it isn't. That program would have been easy to write. What I did was take this defunct educational software company's product and reverse engineer it. The original code embedded in some bullshit essay grading software designed for kids prepping for the SAT. I just switched the analysis functions to output functions, tested the living shit out of it, and now it writes sonnets."

"What would it take for you to teach me your system? I'll pay you, get you pot, whatever," I said.

We haggled back and forth a bit, Kevin declining to teach me his code, me basically begging. It was one of those negotiations that is really about the person with the advantage making the other person grovel and humiliate themselves. Eventually he relented.

"In terms of payment, I want flowers and rainbows, Hallmark cards and Disney videos, bunny rabbits, little bows, puppies, happy things," he said, before he repacked his bong and took another in a series of hits. "Like one of them Whitman Sampler deals. I'm serious, dickhead."

When I told The Fonz and the others that Kevin had slammed his door in my face and wouldn't cough up any info on the code he'd written, the explanation seemed consistent with Kevin's personality, and they quickly moved on to other preoccupations. Kevin had threatened to hack my credit history if I told Optimum Synergies anything, and I believed he could get away with it. Once I excised his freaky lines and performed another round of tweaks, our system ran at 98 percent accuracy, which seemed to please the others. They were happy, and for a while I was the hero.

Between treatments, on an "up" week, Kevin held forth, baked and motormouthed. "Did you know that the fundamental building blocks of life are not cells, are not DNA, are not even carbon but language yeah 'cause DNA is just a four-character language and binary code is a two-character language and what these languages are saying is the very act of revealing, so you reach an X-point when language attains a level of complexity where it begins to fold in upon itself trying to understand itself and this is *sentience*. Did you know that the entire Library of Congress can be encoded in our DNA because all you have to do is translate a binary system into a four-character system to where you can decode the genes like you're searching a microfiche and if you were to genetically engineer the corpus of human knowledge into our DNA then we'd be able to genetically pass the entire library along from generation to generation like a frickin' disease, man."

At home, on a closed network off the grid, I tangled with Kevin's code per our arrangement. It went like this: every week I would perform what he called the Senseless Act of Innocence and Purity, bringing him some small present that was incapable of offending anyone. As long as I kept bringing him gift baskets and sweatshirts with kittens embroidered on them, he burned me discs of his work that I took home to pick apart.

There's this aura that sometimes surrounds techies that what we're doing is some kind of mystical shit, when actually we're merely following processes that actual geniuses invented. Fanning, Wozniak, Kaphan, Case. These were the guys who laid out the terms of the argument, who envisioned the meta-architecture of our tools. The more I learned about Kevin's code the more I knew he belonged in the company of the greats. His scripts and mine were like the difference between Shakespeare and a first grade language textbook. They were almost artful, majestic.

I visited the UW library for articles that would help me understand the groundwork that enabled him to come to his terrifying and paradoxical conclusions—Morgan et al.'s "Stochastic

Perceptual Auditory-Event-Based Models for Speech Recognition," Saunders and Gero's "The Digital Clockwork Muse: A Computational Model of Aesthetic Evolution," Pearce and Wiggins's "Toward a Framework of Evaluation of Machine Compositions," Billinge and Addis's "Some Fundamental Limits of Automated Artistic Decision Making." Deep inside Kevin's code I wondered if I had been immersed beyond my abilities. The voice of my father kept bringing me to the surface, repeating its refrain: So what was it that the system actually did? The answer lay in the 900 square feet of Kevin Wannamaker's condo, where eight networked machines labored at near capacity to produce poems. Unfortunately my knowledge of poetry started and ended with Shel Silverstein, so I was the last person who could judge whether or not the system's poems were any good. To educate myself, I picked up a couple books of poetry every time I checked out a book on linguistics. Mostly stuff any freshman English Lit major would laugh at me for reading, the classics. Whitman, Frost, Shakespeare's sonnets. One night a bored work study library assistant gave me a tour of some cooler stuff: Ginsberg, Ferlinghetti, Corso, Brautigan. Once in a while a line or two would stick, but reading this stuff was painful. It squirted around outside of itself, refused to be pinned into a structure. I wanted to reformat it, preface every line with a command prompt. By the time I hit some contemporaries like Marianne Moore, John Ashbery, and James Tate, I was thoroughly lost, able to extract sense from barely a fraction of it. When I compared what Kevin's system produced to these products of human rapture and suffering, honestly I found it hard to tell a difference. And no one wrote more like a machine than that e.e. cummings guy.

In the background roiled a family melodrama. Starbucks had been making offers to my dad for years. His corner space in a fifty-year-old brick building had been making the company really horny. At first these overtures drew from him outright resistance, but I sensed him growing wearier as the frequency and dollar amount increased.

"We've served free coffee at the store for years," my dad said, pathetically.

When my mom joined the chorus asking him to sell, he sank further into his scuffed easy chair like a retracting growth and said he wasn't ready to retire. What he meant was, he had come to accept that I wasn't going to take over the store, so to punish me he would continue working until all he had left to sell were three screwdrivers and a quart of thinner, if that's what it took to show me the value of a true work ethic.

Finally, during one of our weekly Wednesday family meals, I'd had enough condescension and exploded over the green beans and turkey loaf. "Jesus, Dad. I work fifteen fucking hours a day!"

"Working long hours doesn't equal doing a good job. Doing a good job is about doing something useful for the common man."

"The common man? Dad, you stopped being the common man way before Microsoft even took over the Eastside. The common man doesn't use a ledger. The common man knows how to use a goddamn computer."

"Please," my mother said, but the word didn't have much agency behind it. I stood up, threw down my napkin and headed for the door. She asked where I was going.

"To the office. I have work to do."

But I wasn't really accomplishing much at the office in terms of actual deliverables. When I wasn't placing bids on Beanie Babies and decorative hot pads on eBay for Kevin, I was overtaken with his code, mumbling bits of it without realizing I was mumbling, filling legal pads with transcriptions. Kevin refused to divulge his treatment schedule, so I never knew what kind of condition I'd find him in during my visits. One visit he'd be neurotically adjusting his Witkin prints and the next time he'd be mummified in a down comforter, sweating and groaning. He said water tasted metallic and unbearable. His mouth hurt. His dreams were twisted desecrations of pop culture where he was abused by the Seven Dwarves then transformed into a black guy pursued by Klansmen. It was ugly, toxin-induced stuff that came out of his head, while out of his computers came stanzas of what my layman's mind took to be stunningly well conceived. The poems seemed to be getting better, as if the machine was developing as an artist.

"What do you want me to do with these?" I said, riffling through a stack of print-outs.

"Burn them. Throw them in the Sound. Mulch them for your garden."

Kevin made me swear to never show anyone his system's work, but like any good executor of a literary genius' estate, I defied his will, spiriting his system's poems away when he was too ill to notice or give a damn. I left with reams, storing them in U-Haul moving boxes in my apartment.

At work I went through the motions of repro'ing bugs and moved my equipment to a cubicle in a row gutted empty by lay-offs. In a couple places traces of the cubes' previous inhabitants remained—a half-drunk bottle of soda, some children's pictures tacked to a cube wall. I unscrewed the fluorescent bulbs over my desk and closed the blinds of a nearby window. Occasionally Ralph Malph or Chachi came by to shoot the shit, but my sullen demeanor eventually shooed them away for good. No matter how deeply I penetrated Kevin's code I still could not figure out this miraculous journey between alphanumerics and prose. Slowly I came to suspect that his weekly tips were purposely mis-leading, that he was just fucking with me as a way to get back at Optimum Synergies.

I tried to talk to Kevin about my family, the mom-and-pop hardware business, but he kept fading. I talked anyway, gave him a half-hour history lesson in power tools, and by the time I con-cluded my story in the present, it occurred to me that I knew nothing about Kevin's family, his friends, who was providing him support during his chemo. Then he asked me to kill him.

"I'm not killing you. It's that cocktail of drugs talking."

"I'm completely lucid. They can't chase it out of me fast enough. In another week they're putting me in the hospital until the end. Please do me this favor. Kill me, then destroy all my machines."

"I'll do one, but I won't do the other," I said, then kicked his laptop off the coffee table. "How's that feel, huh Kevin?"

"Yes, erase it all. You're too stupid to crack it anyway."

"There's nothing to crack. Your code is bullshit. Your poetry is meaningless."

"Sell all my stuff. Give it away. Let my mark on this earth be gentle."

A printer nearby spit out some blank verse and blinked for more paper. I quickly tried to remember the status of the assisted suicide laws in Washington state. Kevin had me paralyzed between wanting to strangle him and knowing I would carry him around like a stone in my pocket for the rest of my life. He would have to die by himself.

"What do you want me to do with all this grandmotherly crap you insist on me bringing you?" I said.

"There's a group for kids with leukemia I give it to. I wrote their address on the cover of the phone book."

"Well look who's noble."

"You can't stand it, can you? You got in when the strike prices were low and stuck around long enough to watch the media suck your company's dick. You were convinced you were some hot shit code warrior but now you're starting to understand that your skill set is irrelevant. You never stumbled upon that mythic killer app. You just walk behind the geniuses with your broom tidying up their code. You're like millions of other maladjusted geeks with jobs and shitty apartments and no pussy. So the best thing you can hope to achieve is to suck off some of the bound-lessly revolutionary code that spews effortlessly from my head," Kevin said.

"Revolutionary, yeah. How many people you know read *poems*, Kevin? If you were such a genius you'd figure some slick new way to deconstruct the stock market. The only people inter-ested in reading poetry would flat-out reject poetry written by machines. Poetry is—it's more than what can be constructed by a computer. Poetry is like the source code of human meaning."

"The poems are the byproduct. The real poetry is what the sys-tem actually does to produce the poems, the endless variation of marrying verb with noun with adjective. The system is teaching machines to speak to us. We're going to finally pass the Turing test. Between grammar and meaning there is a depthless chasm and it is into this chasm that my system peers."

"You are so high right now. Like a baked college student in a dorm room."

"I gave you my system as a gift."

"If you wanted to give it as a gift you would have open-sourced the motherfucker instead of doling it out one CD-R at a time."

"You don't understand. I'm just giving it to you as it generates itself. It's the serpent eating its own tail."

Kevin fell into eyelid-twitching sleep. I picked up the laptop I'd kicked, took a blank CD-R from a nearby spindle and slipped it into the drive. Kevin already had his directory view open, so all

131

I had to do was drag and drop. I got everything onto twelve discs while he dreamt.

In a single day, my dad sold his building, I lost my job, and Kevin died. It was one of those run-of-the-mill accidents heard about hundreds of times during the morning commute, narrated from choppers hovering over Interstate 5. Right through the middle of downtown Seattle the freeway shrinks from five lanes to two. This is where Kevin plowed his Audi into a concrete pillar doing 90 miles an hour. It couldn't have been an accident. He'd loaded his car with stuffed animals and dried flowers, as if he were on his way to deliver them to the Fred Hutchinson Cancer Research Center. Had that been the case, however, he wouldn't have taken that particular route. Recreating the last mile and a half of his life in my head, I'm not convinced he left his apartment intent on killing himself. What better suicide note, though, than to upload his system to half a dozen open source advocacy sites. And what more spiteful gesture than to load hundreds of jpegs of kiddie porn to my work machines.

Optimum's HR director, I'll call her Mrs. Cunningham, met me in the lobby to collect my parking pass and tell me how I could extend my health insurance. I went home to vent on fuckedcompany.com and found my inbox full of mail from developers I'd met online, asking if I knew anything about Kevin's accident. My mother left a string of messages on my voicemail wondering if I could help my dad move his remaining inventory into their garage. I bought an armload of malt liquor from a scary mini mart in my neighborhood and drank myself unconscious.

I scroll backward through the months since Kevin died and notice that I had deadlines for freelance work, commitments to my family and the Washington State Employment Security Department, but I remember little of it. After learning I had been named sole beneficiary of Kevin's will, I figured it would be easier just to move into his apartment instead of hauling all his stuff to mine. And while I had first interpreted Kevin's setting me up to lose my job as an act of spite, I slowly began to understand that it was his way of ensuring I would devote my time to maintaining his system in his absence. Even though I use his computers and wear his clothes, I'm just one of thousands of developers who gaze daily into the grand enigma he left us. I recently read a post on a site devoted to his system that said that human achievements occur in explosive bursts. One moment in history a bunch of guys figure out how to forge steel, and it's hardly any time at all before train tracks are being laid across continents and artificial hearts pump in chests. When I'm not managing my dad's sales on eBay I read about all the various ways Kevin's code has insinuated itself into global warming monitoring applications, neurochemistry research, the mathematics of ocean waves. As to whether the poetry his system created is any good, I appear to have been right on that count. The system's verse has been soundly vilified in editorials—and in a couple instances whole books—by America's great literary voices. Kevin seems to have instigated one of those paradigm shifts that asserts its dominance over us by virtue of the sheer amount of controversy it generates. I know of at least one liberal arts school that recently dropped some poetry courses to make room for a whole department devoted to the system. I have been invited to speak at a symposium about Kevin's legacy, cosponsored by The American Society of Poets and MIT's artificial intelligence lab. It's in a week and I haven't started preparing my notes. I have more important things occupying me. I'm on to something that's going to be huge.

The Flautist

I can really bust shit out on the flute. I also play rhythm guitar, bass, and can carry a beat on a trap set. But it's my flute work that's my life blood! My flute-playing talents got me a steady gig at Telempco Pro Recording. They exist off exit 132 across the street from Oak Barn. The building is a no-nonsense cinderblock affair. The miniature-sized Telempco sign faces the alley like it's not legit, but inside studio 1 is a mess of sweaty activity. During our peak we can lay down literally one hundred songs a day. Just set the music in front of me and I can 99 percent of the time nail it in one take.

Lately things have gotten slim, song-wise. You can tell how bad the books are looking by how hard Karl Grobin Jr., our producer and owner of Telempco, rides our collective ass. When his dad ran the place it was like clockwork and we even had a company Christmas party. You felt like you were part of something. You felt like you weren't whoring your musical talents on shitty jingles for discount tire stores. You could take some pride in the blisters and endless night sessions. Junior exhibits what Stu, our tenor sax player, calls a micromanagement management style. He yells at us if we leave a coffee cup on an amp, wastes time arguing microphone placement with the engineers. This has made for a not so healthy creative environment. When the clarinet player was let go, the vibe grew definitely less life-affirming.

So I get to work and am putting a new set of strings on my Gibson hollow body when Junior comes in and starts razzing me about the previous night's session. Seems he's reviewing the take and my flute solo on a number called "Pea Patch Memories" is in the wrong key. Cocksuckingly impossible. That's not what I tell him, mind you; I just say, "Impossible." And to prove my point I paw through the recycling bin and pull out the number in question and show him it was in D.

"That's what I played it in," I say. "If I'm just overdubbing against a click track how the frick am I supposed to know if it's in the same key as the rest of the band? If I'm in the wrong key, man, the writer messed up."

Junior makes some more noise, and I notice a blob of shaving gel under his ear that I decide not to tell him about, just to be spiteful. We both know that if we get in a pissing match about theory he's going to lose, because his own musical career came to a halt when he lost three fingers in a fake crabmeat plant in Alaska and he never had the cojones to pick up the mandolin again. So he storms out of the studio and no doubt heads upstairs to chew out the songwriters, these two dudes and a woman who had to pay for their own coffeemaker because when the old one broke Junior was a cheapass.

In addition to recording jingles and karaoke versions of real songs we have this sideline service called Create-A-Hit, which we advertise in some of the music magazines with the more reasonable advertising rates. Here's how it works: If you have always wanted to hear your lyrics set to music, you just pay us a fee, send us the lyrics and fill out a form and we set it to music and record it with your choice of male or female vocalist. The bronze package ($100) gets you professional guitar backup. Guitar solo? Yes/No. The silver ($150) gets you the addition of bass, drums, and choice of wind instrument. For the gold ($200), you get all the above plus a string section and multiple woodwinds/brass. We can rip through a couple dozen silvers in a day. Sometimes the lyrics are decent. The strings are actually a keyboard, but the woodwinds are real.

No one has ever ordered the Diamond package ($1,000).

Since the Create-A-Hits are cheaper than our commercial and karaoke work, we're expected to spend as little time as possible on them. But I always think of that teenaged girl or lonely old man in his apartment who spent great care penning the words and I try to keep them in mind when I play my parts. Plus, I tend to lay off a lot of the talk that happens around here about the lousy quality of the songs we're playing. If you lose pride in your work you infect your talent with poor quality, and then a terrible spiral of work hatred is created. So I try to keep it upbeat.

Sometimes my patience is tested, however! One of the male vocalists we have on staff, this fellow named Maurice D'Angelo, always gets to me. You can tell he hates himself for taking this gig, that he thinks he belongs on a fully stocked tour bus with video games and free Snapple instead of in a claustrophobic recording booth a stone's throw from the factory where they make the hot sauce. Just because he toured with Hammer's backup band "back in the day," as he likes to remind us, doesn't mean he has to treat us like dog dirt. He's always telling us we're too flat and making jokes that we just woke up, and this just makes me play my flute in an angry, punk rock fashion that I don't think sounds as beautiful.

"How are my boys tonight," Maurice says into the booth mic. He's wearing sunglasses inside. "What piece of musical sausage do we have before us. Looks like a number called 'Rosebud Serenade.' Oh my, rhyming 'fire' and 'desire' in the first verse. Hoo boy this is going to be a long night."

So we get the word from the board that we're all set and Don counts us off. We've been playing together so long we've gotten to that magical zone where you can anticipate where the other guyses fingers are going to land. Mary, our bassist, lays down a line so steady you could've hung laundry from the mother. I'm not hearing Don's part so clearly through the headphones, but that's okay. I just watch his fingers and know where he's going. Carlos our drummer is coming through a little loud. I catch the eye of Larry our engineer and nod my head Carlos's way, then nod down. Soon the volume subsides. Maurice starts in on the song, something about a girl, no, a favorite pet. It is about what a fun time the songwriter used to have with a dog. Then we get to the verse about the beloved companion getting an out-of-

control cyst and having to be euthanized and I think of my own
Corky, a Scottish Terrier I had as a kid. Those sweet memories of
Frisbee play and toys made of wadded up socks make me per-
form with at least twice as much emotion.

One take. Fantastic. In the can.

"Swell job, Franklin," Don says to me, tuning his G. "You
make that instrument sing."

Don is about the only musician in our crew who has a shred
of dignity left to him. Maybe it's because generally he doesn't brag
about all the greats he used to play with even if he could. His
vantage point of twentieth-century popular music is from a stage,
staring at the sequined behinds of a procession of grandiose
divas. He backed them all. On Sundays he hosts a radio show on
the college station that I try to catch. Callers call him and ask nit-
picky questions about different sessions he played on. Like what
brand of strings he was using in 1963. And the crazy thing is,
Don remembers it all.

"Thanks, Don. Nice runs yourself."

At this time, I need to make you all understand the impor-
tance of my particular flute. I grew up being picked on for having a white mom and a black dad. Shitty white-on-the-inside
Oreo cookie comments. But nothing compares to the sneers and
slights I have gotten because of my choice of instrument. You
open a flute case in a crowd of rock and rollers and the eyebrows
get to a level of high. I can't explain the peace I feel pressing my
lips to that cold aperture, or the chills I get hearing one expertly
played. I picked up guitar and drums as a practical move; they're

not where my passion is. And sure, I like classical music, where the flute is generally played, but it's the 4/4 time of rock in which my soul resides! As a youngster I sought any popular tune featuring the flute. (Sometimes, late at night, I put on Snoop Dogg's "Tha Shiznit" just to remind myself that the flute can still be relevant.) Time and again I'd find a flute line in Motown, but then a guy I bought some dope from in high school turned me on to a band that would change my headspace forever, Jethro Tull. I soon amassed, and continue to amass, their entire discography, from *This Was* to *The Broadsword and the Beast* to *J-Tull Dot Com*. The front man, Ian Anderson, not only plays flute well, but he rips on the mother in ways to which I can only hopelessly aspire. The official Tull website says it best: *"Widely recognized as the man who introduced the flute to rock music, Ian Anderson remains the crowned exponent of the popular and rock genres of flute playing. So far, no pretender to the throne has stepped forward."* So true, so very true. Now he owns a salmon farm.

Which brings me to my particular flute. No mere regular flute, it once belonged to Ian Anderson himself and remains my most prized possession. I bid on that sucker on eBay and it came with a hand-signed note from Anderson himself. That my lips touch the instrument that the lips of the creator of the classic "Thick as a Brick" once touched fills me with a power I can't quite wrap my head around.

We bust through eight more songs before Maurice starts making what are known as passive-aggressive comments about his voice, like, "Man, starting to feel scratchy down there. But back when I sang with Hammer we just kept right on rehearsing. You just got to reach down and find that place in your soul where the song resides. I've got another twenty songs in me, easy."

"Singing? With Hammer? More like backup lip-syncing," Don says out of range of his mic.

We lay down five more songs. They are love songs, mostly, except for one about dolphins. It isn't even noon yet.

My girlfriend is fine with the fact that I often work late, because she works late, too. We rarely see each other, but when we do, it's 110 percent magic. One night after recording fifty-eight songs I come back to the apartment, heat me up a pot pie, and sit down in front of some home improvement channel. Those redone bedrooms tend to inspire me. Juanita comes home early, tosses her purse at the couch and absconds to the bathroom, where she yells at me to bring some refill toilet paper. Sitting on the edge of the tub listening to her pee, I start telling her about how much I hate the male vocalists—Maurice, Gary, Scotty—how they try to tell us how to play even though they don't know diddly about arrangement, how we had to waste eight takes on some restaurant jingle because Maurice wasn't "feeling the love."

It's an awfully long pee for Juanita, which makes sense as she works in bars. She's not a bartender, but gets paid to go to bars and order certain brands of liquor, then mingle with the crowd and tell people how much she's enjoying the brand. This week it was Bacardi Silver, and even though she was supposed to nurse her drinks she had been coming home kind of hosed.

I'm one of those guys who says about his girlfriend, "I don't know what she sees in me!" That's what I call an honest emotion of mine. While my self-esteem tends to be in the category of low, I have been told that I combine the best features of my black father and Jewish mother—his cheekbones, her penetrating eyes. Maybe Juanita is attracted to me because of the whole bohemian musician mystique. It's true we met when I was filling in on six string for a mutual friend's acid jazz outfit. For a brief moment her fickle music taste intersected with my spotty professional resume, and we fell hard for each other. If anything breaks us apart it's going to be her nocturnal metabolism and my choice of instrument. Even though we remain dynamite in the hay, she still introduces me to her crew as a guitarist.

Which makes it even more surprising that sitting there midstream she tells me she bragged about my flute prowess to a bunch of guys from the band Storm of Horses.

"They're in town recording their new album. The lead singer guy Conrad says they're experimenting with a bunch of different instruments this time. Timbales, African percussion, bagpipes. I told him I had a friend who was a killer flautist. He told me to give you this."

Juanita fishes from her deliberately distressed jeans a coaster with a name and a phone number written drunkenly within the border of a heart. Okay.

"A heart?" I say.

"Oh, that's the wrong one. Here. This is the right one."

"You told them I was a friend, or your boyfriend?"

Juanita sighs. "Again? This? Baby, you know it makes it easier to advertise the product if customers think I'm available."

"I know. I just had a lousy day at work."

Juanita touches my hair. "I think this could be a great opportunity for you. They have a video on MTV2."

"Hey, I've been on MTV," I say, and it's true; I was man-in-the-street interviewed once for *The Week in Rock* regarding Puffy's name change.

Upon which Juanita falls asleep, her head against the wall, her panties stretched like the Golden Gate Bridge between her knees, if the Golden Gate Bridge had satanic-looking kittens painted all over it. I lift her up and wrestle her garments back to where they're supposed to be. It's then that I notice a fresh, inflamed tattoo of the Storm of Horses logo, the one with an anatomically correct stallion emerging from a cloud, situated right above Juanita's butt crack.

The next day I get hit by a fricking minivan. I'm on my way to work, crossing 43rd Avenue thanks to the little blue man walking light. I don't hear anything. No squealing tires, horn, etc. When the minivan hits me I don't feel pain really, but something bigger and more badass than pain, a jarring sensation that tells me: your body *is*. Like I am made aware of the primacy of my physical self by God. The man upstairs is saying, *That's all you is, sucka: bones and skin.* I'm looking up at clouds and I understand this to be the sky. I understand this when I strike the pavement. Again: your body *is*. I hear my flute case skidding across the street. The orange from my sack lunch lands on my chest. I only become frightened when I realize I can't move. There is a halo of heads gathered around me. Slowly, then, I sit up.

"Whoa, take it easy, mister." It's an EMT who looks like that one guy from that one show. He seems excited to use the stretcher and foam neck brace.

"I think I'm okay," I say. I find that my legs, sort of on their own, decide to put me in a standing position.

"Jesus, Jeffrey, you can't let him walk around like that," says another EMT, approaching from the ambulance.

"I think I'm fine," I say, and my hands are checking my head, my chest. Doesn't feel like I'm bleeding anywhere.

I understand that I'm in the middle of the intersection, with traffic halted on all sides. As a courtesy gesture, I turn to each clod of vehicles and give them a thumbs-up. A couple people honk, and I can't tell if it's because they're aggravated for the delay or happy for my not being dead.

"Let's get you into the ambulance," the other EMT says, and it seems like a ridiculous suggestion, but I know it will make for less hassle so I climb into this kind of submarine-seeming area with all the equipment and supplies.

At the hospital they run me through all sorts of tests. I can tell I am disappointing them by not being more injured. They puzzle over my chart and shrug. After about five, six hours of this, the doctor comes in, looking like a guy who is only dressed as a doctor.

"The police tell me that the van was going about thirty," the doctor says. "You look to be unscathed. You should consider yourself lucky."

"What about my flute?" I say.

The doctor hangs his head. "I'm afraid your flute didn't make it. You can pick it up at the front desk."

"I need to see it," I say, getting out of the bed, fetching my clothes from the closet. It's not like the doctor can argue with me. Dressed, I approach the nurses' station and ask to see my flute. They hand it to me in a box that used to store catheters. The case is shattered, in many pieces, and the flute itself is flattened, like a condom not worn. Standing there looking at my Ian Anderson flute crushed like a roadkill snake (that happens to be decorated with Celtic engravings), I naturally start to cry.

"Oh, babe, I'm so sorry!" It's Juanita, just then beside me at the nurses' station. She says she came as soon as she heard about my accident, but she had to have someone drive her here as she'd been drinking for her job. Her mascara is smeary-looking, and for a second I think that's because she's been crying for my potentially being dead. But then I see that the five other people she is with also have such smeary mascara, and they can't have been crying for me because I have never met them before.

Then I'm hit with a massive déjà vu. I have stood here before, talking to these guys, and I know they are Storm of Horses, and that they'll ask if I was able to score any cool drugs because of my accident, and when I say no they will say that's too bad but do you want to hang out with us tonight because Juanita here says you're a wicked flautist. And then I'll show them my busted flute and they'll say that they think there's one at the studio I can use.

And that's pretty much how it happens, except instead of "wicked" flautist they say "killer."

So I find myself in a kind of van or SUV, and I can hear Juanita sniffing a powdered drug off the bassist's wrist in the back seat. I understand this immediately as a sign that she has had sex with perhaps multiple members of this band. I also know that in the future I will no longer be employed by Telempco, that a smashed flute once owned by Ian Anderson has about zero resale value on eBay, and that tonight, in a darkened studio, surrounded by experimental music I don't understand, I will begin the process of dismantling my own brain.

The studio appears from a cloud of fast food smoke and laughter and we exit the van and ride a sort of wave of loud conversation and exclamations and conspiracy in through the lobby with its cigarette burn armrest couches and gold record walls. Apparently Storm of Horses has booked this studio indefinitely, and it's costing them $1,000 a day. There's a room with food and video games and furniture where various people make out, and there's the actual studio where the producer, who looks maybe fourteen years old, is banging on a couple laptop computers.

Conrad slips his arm around me. "Check this out. Two G4's and a just-out-of-the-box G5 desktop all networked and running a bootleg beta of the next ProTools release. Welcome to the candy store, baby. Fuckin' dozen vintage amps, pedals, we got your like African drums and shit. We got the fuckin' Mellotron action if the mood strikes us. We had to rent a U-Haul just for the rhythm section. Hey Kyle, we have a flute around here somewhere, right?

Can you get one for my bro here? I'm thinking we could add a flute track to 'Erogenous Mouth.'"

Then I'm looking through the window of the control booth and I can see Juanita through panes of soundproof glass with a bottle of Bacardi Silver, gesturing to its label, and then the keyboard player slips his hand under her shirt and she doesn't seem to mind. I want to put my head in a vice and crush it like that old horror movie *The Fly*. But I'm being steered to some place behind a mic, and headphones are being slipped onto my head. Then Conrad, the singer, comes into the booth with a notebook and a metal briefcase, which he opens to display an assortment of pharmaceuticals. I've been around drug scenes before, done dope and fell off a pier once, even snorted blow a couple times before a gig. But these guys are like scientists of drugs. Conrad shows me his notebook, which details in precise amounts the drugs Storm of Horses have ingested going back three albums. There are little charts showing what songs were jammed on while on certain drugs, graphs indicating fluctuations in usage, and even some chemical formulas. It's like he went to college in how to get wasted. He's showing me little vials of this and droppers of that and I want to cry because I know I'm going to take something and it's going to end up with me hunched over a toilet with attractive sober people laughing at me. Then I'm watching Juanita again, or rather I can just see her legs in the position of up as she is on a couch behind where the producer is tweaking tracks, and I point to something in a pretty bottle and say, "I'll take a bit of that."

A little white capsule goes onto my tongue. Conrad suggests I chill for about twenty minutes before I start playing. The flute is offered to me by Kyle, the young producer, and I find it is a well-scuffed and used instrument, an artifact bearing the imprint of many hands. I pet it like an animal, letting it know that I will use it only for the purposes of beauty, not take it for granted or demean its intrinsic delicateness. I imagine that it responds to me, letting me know it has been much abused and not well taken care of. It is scared. I clean and buff it using the oil and cloth in the case, and it grows warm to my touch. And in caring for the instrument I find I am no longer wielding a singular flute, but the fundamental flute of the ages.

"I am a flautist," I say into the microphone.

"Right on," says Kyle's voice. "Let me know when you're ready."

"Go ahead."

The music slowly accumulates in my headphones. It's in some strange time signature, and includes a very creative use of bells. There is a bass line in there somewhere low in the mix, and a hint of vocals. There are these little electronic squishy noises, and I think of the fact that we're destroying sweet Mother Earth. Trucks and cars and airplanes clogging the air, fouling the streams with our chemical spills, hurting all the precious little salamanders. I want to lament the putridity my civilization has bitch slapped the earth with, I want to apologize to the minerals and plants and animals on behalf of the human race, and that's what comes out of my flute, a hellish mournful wail.

The next fourteen hours are like a first-person shooter game, with my new flute held before me as I roam in bubble motion down smoky, telescoping hallways, watching my hand reach for a cocktail, cornered by various band mates with drippy makeup, devolving into a very intense conversation about old Saturday morning cartoons with Pete the drummer which ends with both of us embracing and crying deeply, instigating an honest to God conga line, smoking two cigarettes at once against my better judgment.

The next time I understand what a clock is about, it's a whole day and one-half hour later. Various human forms are sleeping in the couch/video game room. Empty bottles of Bacardi Silver sit upon many a surface. I find Conrad and his notebook, asleep on a yoga mat near the bathroom. I pry the notebook from his hand and flip to the section detailing my name and see a list of horrible shit I put into my body in the past twenty-four hours.

I find Juanita curled on a couch in the lobby, with some metal band's gold record clutched to her chest. She is wearing her leather jacket with no shirt or bra on underneath. I place two fingers on her forehead and say quietly, "Juanita, we had some wicked swell times together. We walked in the moonlight of a moonlit night. We ate really excellent Mexican food together from time to time, and saw some high-quality movies. We freaked nasty for many a special occasion. But now I must go, with this flute as my beacon, and you must join the life of groupies, as it is your one true destiny."

Juanita mumbles something in her sleep and turns over to her other side, exposing a boob. A boob I know I will no longer touch. With the battered old flute in hand, I leave the studio and emerge into a sober world of broken engagements, unforgivable acts, and disappointment. It's dark out, of course, and I have no car. I catch a northbound bus with no intention of going back to my apartment, where I will find all sorts of things to remind me that I just broke up with my unconscious girlfriend. I am the only passenger on the bus, and I sit in back, playing my instrument softly. I consider not prying it from my lips for twenty-four hours straight, just jam on it consistently. It seems like a religious repentance type concept, like something you'd read about in *National Geographic*. You know, that freaky tribe that flays their backs with whips made of virgins' hair and play the flute nonstop until they have visions. I could dig living in a culture like that.

The Sales Team

The last Thursday of every month the sales team meets in the McDonald's across the street, in a room that's usually reserved for little kid birthday parties. Instead of chairs there are these child-sized saddles on posts at all the tables. We sit there like a bunch of cowboys, it's worth a few stale jokes every time. Gart Henderson always places his inflatable hemorrhoid donut on his saddle before he can sit on it. Nobody gives him shit about it because he consistently puts up good numbers. We're talking win-the-Caddy numbers. And hey—there are some interesting parallels in this story I'm about to recount with *Glengarry Glen Ross,* that 1992 Mamet film. Every salesman should see it. Full disclosure: what I'm about to tell you is pretty much a carbon copy of that flick, so if you've seen it there's probably not that much new for you here, except in *Glengarry Glen Ross* there's no attempted rape.

True to this ripped-off plot, our story opens at the last sales meeting when a new guy from corporate showed up. We all sat in our saddles eating our McMuffins and hash browns. The company covered the bill for anything you wanted for breakfast as long as you didn't waste any food. Sometimes new guys went overboard, ordered twice as many pancakes as they were prepared to eat, but I always went easy, got just a parfait and one of those litigiously hot coffees. We had all learned our lesson one morning when Dean Beesmith ordered five breakfast croissants, three orders of sausage, four hash browns, and a couple orders of pancakes. Management had refused to dismiss us that morning until Dean finished the whole meal. Weeping, Dean had choked down the last of his hash browns, then promptly vomited, and everyone had laughed.

Matthias Garvey was the corporate guy's name. His red hair and eyebrows looked like they'd been groomed at a chick salon. True to form he opened his talk with some bullshit metaphor/story.

"The Vikings ruled and plundered the Atlantic from roughly 800 to 1169 A.D.," Garvey said. "When you think of Vikings you probably think about those helmets with the horns. That's just some cartoon bullshit slapped onto the mythology from bad Wagner productions. The Vikings had no use for the trappings of opera. Let's not mince words—they went fucking apeshit in battle and raped the fuck out of all those villages. But the Viking spirit was more, much more. They were skilled litigators who founded Europe's first parliamentary government. They were poets, masters of *kenning,* a complex form of poetry where multiple meanings were packed into each line. They were farmers, cultivating crops in the harshest conditions. My ancestors rode with Leif Erickson and I'm proud of my Viking heritage. And since I can't go out in boats and go berserk on innocent Irish villagers, I decided on a career in sales. Sales encompasses all the elements of the Viking personality. We're negotiators, talking through problems and getting to resolutions. We're poets, spinning our pitches. We're farmers, cultivating our leads. And yes, when we hear the call, we get out there and fucking kill."

Robinson, one of the newer guys, smirked.

"I'm sorry, did you have something to contribute?" Garvey said.

Oh shit Robinson, you dumbass, don't bite.

"Whatever," Robinson said. "Vikings, farmers, okay that's your shtick. But what's your point? Is this story time or something? I don't know about the rest of you guys but I've got leads to follow."

Garvey walked across the room to his briefcase, from which he extracted a Smith and Wesson Model 36, and shot Robinson in the head. The body slumped forward, the head smacking Formica. I had learned from Holocaust movies that bullet wounds to the head gurgle blood out in thick, rhythmic streams, and this head wound did not disappoint. As other sales reps nervously adjusted their ties, I watched the puddle spread and quickly subsume the paper place mat on Robinson's tray. The place mat featured a crossword puzzle, which Robinson had gotten halfway through. Something about it made me incredibly sad, the idea of leaving this earth with a crossword puzzle half-done.

"This year we're going about things a bit differently," Garvey said, as if he needed to. "Instead of every man for himself, we're forming teams of three reps each. Everything you sell goes into the pot you share with the other guys and is split evenly at the end of each month."

There were some further details about who was assigned to each team. We crammed our breakfasts quickly into our silent mouths. On my way out I heard Garvey offer a disingenuous apology to the sullen teenager tasked to clean up after us. I have never disposed of a dead body, but I did flip burgers for a summer, and I know how thankless those kinds of jobs can be.

The other two members of my team were Lucky Mulligan and Grant Bertrand. Lucky had a reputation (or a series of lies that had grown disproportionately into legend) for sleeping with his female clients. That's not why he was called Lucky; his parents had actually given him the name. Lucky was the kind of guy who removed his wedding ring before he went barhopping. He wasn't lecherous by appearance; in fact he had this sort of aw-shucks, boyish aura that was his instant ticket to trim. After breakfast at Mickey D's, we convened in the parking lot at my Benz. Lucky called shotgun and offered me a slice of Big Red as he fiddled with the radio, fucking up the presets.

Grant entered the back of my car and unloaded his sweaty-smelling briefcase onto the seat beside him, rummaging for something cryptic and asinine. He was a big guy. When shaking on a bet, he'd adjust his hand in a creepy way and say, "Let me get my whole mitt in there." It was supposed to be some sort of self-deprecating jab at his freakish physiology, but what he actually meant by the comment was this: I have a really, really, really, really, really big dick.

"Pretty interesting what happened back there at the double arches," Grant said. "I might go so far as to say 'intense.'"

"The speech?" Lucky said.

"It's all about the teamwork," Grant said.

"Fuck you," I said, "and the Successory where that came from."

"Who's first on the lead list?" Lucky said.

We consulted the paperwork we'd been provided, generated from the database of some malevolent and all-seeing deity. I recognized the address as being in a part of town where people generally didn't have much disposable income. I knew we were doomed. Grant shook some yellow pills into his fist and distributed them among us. "Don't be a chickenshit," he said. "This is what the Marines are taking before they go on raids in Iraq."

The pill seemed to have no effect except to make me acutely aware that my leather steering wheel cover had once belonged to a living being, I'm betting a cow. So porous, so flesh-like! We found the first house on the list, found it condemned. I drove, injecting us further into what we called the red-light district for lack of a more creative term. The places you went to blow money, to buy blow, to get blown. It was noon.

"I don't know about you fellas," Lucky said, "but I was sorely disappointed to learn that a table dance doesn't mean the stripper actually dances on your table."

Stopped at a light in front of a third-tier mini mart, I observed a parking lot drug transaction going down. The dealer, a Vietnamese guy in a quilted jacket and backward baseball hat like he was auditioning for the part, performing this sort of shoulder-rolling approach to the buyer, a Latino guy in an army jacket. Bills and a little brown vial were exchanged. In another era and continent the dealer would have been a shaman and the deal would have been culturally okay. It would have happened in a tropical setting instead of in front of an on-the-fritz Budweiser sign. Nonetheless, the exchange struck me as primal and honest. I pulled into the parking lot and rolled down my window.

"Hey, young entrepreneur. What's for sale today?"

The dealer glanced sideward, betraying reservations.

"Come on, I'm not a cop. And if I was, I'd have to tell you. That's the law, at least as I understand it."

"What do you faggots want?"

"I want to give you some advice," I said. "You're wasting your time dealing down-market crack in a mini mart parking lot. I guarantee every motorist who passes knows you're dealing. And while you may think that grants you greater visibility, it works to your disadvantage; your customers are no doubt hesitant to be seen in your presence. You're in one of the poorest neighborhoods in the city. We're salesmen, we've seen the demographic data, we know our shit. As a private entity you're in the enviable position to go where the money is, and it's not here. It's on college campuses, where kids living off mom and dad are just sitting around downloading music, reading freaked out French philosophy, horny, and always on the lookout for any opportunity to get loaded. So if you really want to set yourself apart in the dealing game, enroll in a community college for a year or two, work hard, get solid grades, then transfer to a four-year school where you'll find a dope-hungry customer base and hotter chicks than the skanks in this neighborhood."

As I spoke, the dealer's shoulders lowered and his face softened until he resembled exactly what he was, a kid.

"Who are you guys? Fuckin' social workers?" he said.

"We're salesmen," I said. "Modern-day Vikings, if you will. You carry a piece?"

The guy opened his jacket, lifted his shirt, and revealed the grip of a beautiful gun.

"How much you want for it?" I said, pulling out my money clip, peeling back fifties. The kid parted with it for three hundred bucks. As we drove away I stuffed it inside my jacket pocket. "One more gun off the streets," I said.

"Just doing our part for the community," Lucky said.

Somehow, somewhat to my surprise, I found myself inhabiting a land betrayed by God. This I have never known as acutely as when I discovered myself, forty years old, lugging my weight from one unconsummated transaction to another in my leased Benz, high as hell and packing heat with a couple of other wiseass salesmen. We knew the team approach to selling was antithetical to the deepest needs of our salesmanship DNA, that we'd been set up to fail by Garvey or whoever lubed Garvey's asshole way up in the higher echelons of commerce where the metaphysical decisions are handed down. Damned. That's who we were and what had been done to us. Look at us, with our big gold class rings as if anyone gave a fuck. Listen to our language of steak dinners and commissions and the Miller-Hyman Sales Probability Index. I'm not kidding here that we had been turned into something despicable and unworthy of love and we had no one but ourselves to hate.

With the darkening road lit by twin phalluses of automobile light we passed around a little pipe fashioned from aluminum foil into which something white was poured, ignited, inhaled. And when we got to the last house on our list Lucky grabbed me and Grant by the shoulders and said, "Whatever you do, if there's a woman in the house, please don't rape her, okay? Will you promise me that? Please?"

We made sounds of agreement and I jogged up the steps to the porch and knocked. Some college professor-looking man answered and asked what we needed.

"We were wondering if we could have a few minutes of your time to tell you a little bit about our product, on which, for a limited time, we're offering a deep discount."

"We're eating dinner."

"Smells good," Grant said, pushing the door open, stepping around the guy.

"What's your name?" I said.

"Jonathan. Please. We don't want to be disrupted."

I watched Grant walk down the hall toward a bright, yellow kitchen. There was some sort of art on the wall that looked like it had been hung upside down. As Jonathan the professor protested our entrance, my ears filled with white noise and garbage and I found myself transported into the dining room where Jonathan's wife and daughter sat stiffly before plates of dinner from which Grant was picking as he delivered his pitch. I knew Grant wouldn't go for the mom, but the daughter worried me. A teenager, she looked like she belonged to lots of clubs at school. I could tell Lucky was having the same thoughts I was, as he had placed himself between the girl and Grant, and was bent over, whispering something into her ear that elicited no response but a frozen expression of terror and a trembling lower lip. Lucky was trying to reassure her that we wouldn't hurt anyone, but whatever he was saying wasn't all that convincing. A tear slid down the girl's cheek, landing in her au gratin potatoes.

"Please. Just leave our house," Jonathan begged me, gently touching my arm. I jerked out of the way and threw him against a wall, knocking down a collectible plate we'd unfortunately have to deduct from our cut of the sale.

"Just chill! The fuck! Out!" I yelled. "Is this how you treat guests in your house?"

"Hey fellas," Grant said, "I just noticed something odd here. I see four place settings."

"Upstairs," I said, "I'll check it out."

I sprinted to the second floor and scanned the bedrooms. At the end of the hall I found a teenage guy in the process of climbing out his window. I grabbed him by the belt and yanked. He fell against his desk, scattering baseball trophies and CDRs.

"Don't hurt me. Don't hurt my family." A patch of piss spread in the crotch of his jeans.

"Jesus Christ," I said, "we're *salesmen*. Just come downstairs and listen to our special introductory offer."

As we reached the top of the stairs, one of the females screamed in the dining room below. To get the kid moving, I flashed my gun, which made him immediately vomit over the railing. Half-dragging him by the collar, I entered the dining room to find Grant sitting on the chest of the daughter trying to undo her blouse. Lucky stood over them, trying to talk him out of it. "This isn't funny, Grant. This is a completely real, horrible thing you're contemplating doing here."

"Shut the fuck up and make sure the dad doesn't get loose."

Both parents were wailing hysterically. I was disappointed we hadn't even gotten to the point where we could talk about the tiered savings schedule. The son's knees buckled and he fell to the floor, a blubbering mess. There was no way Lucky was going to pull a guy Grant's size off the girl. I aimed vaguely at her chest and fired.

"You prick!" Grant roared.

"You weren't getting off her," I said. "While you're wasting your time with the daughter, the two principal financial decision makers of the household are just sitting here while you could be giving them the pitch!"

Two or three cop cars pulled up outside. I threw my hands up in exasperation. "Okay, who called the police?" I kicked the boy, a light tap, really, but one that caused him to erupt in new tears. "It was you, wasn't it? Okay, well, I guess I'll get the door."

I opened the front door on a phalanx of officers who had their guns drawn. I held my gun out butt-first, which they quickly confiscated. "We're just salesmen!" I said, and this seemed to put them all at ease. Their weapons made their way back to their holsters. A sergeant of some sort stepped forward and I led him to the dining room, where Grant was wiping blood off his face with a corner of the table cloth, and Lucky was in mid-pitch with the ashen-faced mom.

"What's going on here?" the officer said, glancing at the dead girl.

"We're salesmen," Grant said, "and these folks have been uncooperative the whole time we've been here."

"We've been treated very rudely," Lucky said.

"And the girl here," the sergeant said, "she resist?"

"I had to shoot her because my colleague was trying to rape her," I said.

"Sort of an honor-defending thing," Lucky said.

"Then I suppose you can carry on," the officer said, then stooped to address the boy. "And I suppose you're the young man who placed the 911 call. I'm going to let you off this time, but next time you make an erroneous call I'm afraid we'll have to write you up a ticket."

I thanked the officer and his backup for their time and showed them the door. When I returned to the dining room, Jonathan had puked down the front of his shirt. Grant had moved on to the mother. Lucky was speaking in exasperated tones to the boy. "I don't know who you people think you are, but we have a *product*. What do you even have?"

I picked up Jonathan's glasses from the plate of food they had fallen into, wiped off some cream sauce, then placed them back on his face. "Now," I said, "you're really going to like our new deferred payment plan."

Absolut
Boudinot

We were the first major terrorist group to strike on Halloween. Why no other terrorist organization had thought of it first, we couldn't fathom. Halloween provided the perfect cover for our plan. We would all dress as clowns, the six of us, in a rented U-Haul, our identities obscured from surveillance of any kind. This year Halloween fell on a Friday. There were Halloween parties all over the city that night, and we knew to expect many drunken revelers and lax security across the board.

Dressed as clowns, we parked the U-Haul in front of the Federal Court House. Part of our plan, using the cover of the night in addition to our costumes, meant that collateral damage would be minimal. We preferred it that way. We weren't the kinds of terrorists interested in killing lots of people. We sought to destroy property and if the security guard inside bit it, hey, too bad so sad.

The garbage cans of fertilizer in the back of the first U-Haul did the trick and reduced the Federal Court House to rubble. Unfortunately a procession of limousines ferrying teenagers to a formal dance happened to be driving past the U-Haul as the timer detonated the charge. And we had forgotten to factor in the convent, chock full of nuns, across the street from our target. It, too, fell with the blast. Then there was the Humane Society and Homeless Shelter on the other side of the building that had escaped our notice. Oh well, that's one of the costs of doing our part to avenge Big Government and Homosexual Rights.

When the building came down we were several blocks away, at our favorite bar, enjoying a round of Absolut Citron martinis. Our brightly painted lips curled around the sugared edges of the stemware, leaving smudges of greasepaint. Greg, the bartender, had made them just right, with a dash of Angostura bitters and a sugared lemon wedge rather than an olive. As the sound of emergency vehicles filled our ears, we raised our glasses to toast the destruction of decadent Western civilization and a job well done.

So Little Time

Our plan was to save that summer's bulb-picking money to spend on tickets, refreshments, and collectibles at the *Dr. Who* convention in August.

Picking bulbs sucks donkey ass.

It sucks for the junior pickers who spend all day dragging their butts through the furrows. Sucks for the high school–aged checkers who go rake the hell out of your row to make sure you didn't miss any bulbs. It even sucks for the senior-level pickers who are allowed to listen to Walkmen. After the third day or so of picking, holes start appearing in your gloves and when you blow your nose mud comes out. Five days a week, from seven in the morning to four in the afternoon. Sitting on bare ground, eating Hostess fruit pies with dirty hands. We got paid by the foot, the rate depending on the type of bulb, but never over eight cents. I could usually complete two 200-foot rows per shift. That's $8 a day for irises, which might not sound like much, but over a summer it adds up to a lot of money to blow at a science fiction convention.

Two things that made this job bearable were my friends Raul and Chris. Some days, if we were lucky, the weather would turn and the grown-up supervisors at Turner Farms would drive an empty semi trailer out to the field where all us kids would wait out the rain. There were some other benefits—if you stayed on for the whole season, you got a bonus check for 10 percent of your summer's earnings. At the end of the summer Turner Farms promised to buy us each a hamburger and small fry from McDonald's, with our choice of canned soda. The senior pickers were also to get hot apple pies. Raul, Chris, and I knew we'd never become senior pickers. You had to pick 600-plus feet a day for a whole season to earn the rank. We were content to work side by side, keeping pace with each other so that we'd finish our rows at the same time, and thus stay together when we got assigned to a new section of the field.

Raul's dad was an ear doctor, his mother a teacher, but they made him work in the fields just as they had when they were kids. In the living room of their house was a framed picture of Raul's grandparents with their arms around César Chávez. Mr. and Mrs. Vasquez never neglected to tell me that guy's whole life story every time I visited. They made Raul work in the fields as a stay-connected-to-your-roots thing, even though they spoiled him in every other aspect of his life.

Raul's super power? He knew the Marvel universe better than anyone with whom I was acquainted. As a gesture of his fandom, he had duct-taped some tongue depressors from his dad's office to his gloves to simulate the talons of his favorite super hero, Wolverine from X-Men. He claimed they helped him pick bulbs faster.

"You're so full of shit, Vasquez," Chris said. "If they make you pick faster, how come you can barely get 400 feet a day like the rest of us turds?"

"No, he actually does pick faster," I said. "He needs the talons to keep up with us."

Raul threw a bulb at Chris and was immediately reprimanded by a checker. One didn't start a bulb fight with Chris Peterson. The guy could throw harder and faster than anyone in my grade, a talent that would later land him a dead-end career on a minor league farm team for the Pittsburgh Pirates. He had other talents, too. He could recite the entire alphabet within a single belch. His mustache was a thing to which we all aspired. I'd watched him slowly hit himself in the nose sixty-eight times until it bled. That flip-up-the-eyelids trick—Chris practically invented it. But his primary super power was that his parents let him see R-rated movies, most recently *Conan the Barbarian*. I frequently had him recount the humping scene with the witch who shoots fireballs.

My problems? You mean besides the fact that my name is Dick Dills?! My problem was that I had asthma and two parents who pretty much looked exactly like the parents in *Family Circus*. Other problems included a little brother who ate the wheels off my Stompers, and the tendency to get boners on days when I wore sweatpants to school.

This was the summer after seventh grade. We walked with the swagger of those who knew they were three months away from completely ruling a junior high school.

One afternoon we waved our hats and three checkers came off their smoke breaks to pick at the mounds of dirt for the bulbs we'd missed. Tragically, I got assigned the most feared checker at Turner Farms, this bitch named Lucinda Owens, known to force kids to smell her unshaved armpits. Relentlessly, she hacked at the butt prints I had left on my row, unearthing clumps of iris bulbs. About ten feet in she spat phlegm and demanded that I go over my row again. That this would impede my ability to hit the 400-foot mark for the day didn't distress me as much as that I would be separated from my friends. I watched sadly as Chris and Raul's checkers joked and flirted with them, poking haphazardly at the ground with their picks. Lucinda relit a bent-in-half Pall Mall she'd sort of repaired with a mini Band-Aid.

"We'll try to save you a row," Raul said, passing me on his way to a more eventful section of the field.

"Later days, better lays," Chris said, his boilerplate farewell.

I completed the row, satisfied Lucinda's probing eye, and ended up on the side of the field opposite my friends. Worse, my new row was between the rows of two high school girls named Brandy and Gwendolyn. They were faster pickers than me, which allowed me the benefit of furtive ass viewings.

"I don't know what's sicker, that she perioded through her pants in the first place or that she just sat in it all day," Gwendolyn said.

Brandy adjusted the neck of her International NEWS sweatshirt, purposely revealing a bra strap, and said, "So what are you doing this weekend?"

"I don't know," Gwendolyn said. "Probably walking around my house naked all day."

Both girls glanced over their shoulders to see if their conversation was having the intended effect on me. I tried to concentrate on digging through the clods of dirt and dropping the bulbs in the bucket. My chest started hitching up. My inhaler was in my left breast pocket. I waited for a moment when both girls were looking away to grab it.

"I love being naked," Brandy said, "I could play with my nipples for hours."

"Yeah, me too," Gwendolyn said, "I especially like my pubic hair."

My head tilted to one side and stayed there, cocked. I wanted to return it to an upright position, but it was like my ear had turned into a suction cup stuck to my shoulder. When Gwendolyn and Brandy started to laugh, I found I could no longer breathe. Then, vomiting into my bulb bucket, I passed out.

When I came to the girls had completed their rows and were rattling off a series of Valley Girl repulsion synonyms. A checker named Randy splashed a Dixie cup of water in my face.

"How come you didn't aim for the ground, pissant?" Randy said. "Now these bulbs are ruined! Shee-it!"

Then they honked the truck horn three times and we knew it was time to gather our lunch coolers and go home.

My father, Russ, was looking forward to the *Dr. Who* convention as much as my friends and me. Saturday nights we'd watch the show, broadcast from a station located close to the Canadian border. You could never tell what country they were trying to appeal to. They'd run the French-English version of Sesame Street and deliver the weather reports in centigrade.

"Exterminate! Exterminate! Exterminate!" my father barked in the frantic robot-inflections of Dr. Who's great nemeses, the Daleks. He'd become enamored with this catchphrase and showed no signs of retiring it. Trimming the hedges, he'd yell, "Exterminate!" Sweeping the garage: "Exterminate!" Muscling the lid off a jar of pickles: "Exterminate!"

The cool thing about *Dr. Who* was that each episode was at least two hours long. Sometimes longer. In the UK, they serialized the episodes into half-hour sub-episodes and showed them over the course of a month. With episodes going back to the sixties, the *Dr. Who* universe was an endlessly fertile system of shitty special effects with which we stoked our imaginations.

One night I invited Raul and Chris over for a special viewing of the episode in which Dr. #4, played by Tom Baker, dies and regenerates into Dr. #5, played by Peter Davison. We knew this episode was coming, as we'd read the novelizations and episode guide. We shared the ambivalence of knowing that our favorite Dr. Who was about to step off stage in a really dramatic manner, as we all agreed that Baker's Who, with his freakishly long scarf, white man 'fro, and floppy hat, was the definitive Dr., and we'd be sad to see him pass the torch.

I heard the Vasquezes' Cadillac pull into the driveway and met Raul at the door. In each arm he held a two-liter bottle of Mountain Dew. "Who's ready to party?" he said.

While my mom prepared dinner, we waited for Chris, fearing he wasn't going to make it. I didn't want to get started without him.

"Why don't you call him and let him know we'll save some tacos for him if he's a little late," my mother said.

"His family doesn't have a phone," I said.

"Oh, right," my mom said.

Oftentimes Chris would be the one to end a discussion with a reminder of his family's poverty. One time in fifth grade our teacher, Mrs. Hregvidson, organized a Valentine's Day party and asked everyone to sign up to bring something. I signed on for the plastic ware. I think Raul agreed to bring cider. When Mrs. H. asked Chris what he'd like to bring, he sat slouched in his desk/chair combo with this unimpressed expression. "I can't bring anything."

"How about napkins?" Mrs. H. said.

"We don't have any money," Chris said.

"Surely you can afford to bring napkins."

Chris banged his fist on his desk and shouted, "I'm poor! I'm poor! I'm poor!"

It was the only time I had ever seen a teacher not reprimand a kid for yelling in class. We all uncomfortably returned to diagramming sentences, and those of us who were Chris's friends whispered incredulously among ourselves at Mrs. H.'s insensitivity as she hurriedly watered a sprouting avocado seed. Bad judgment call on her part. Chris's family's poverty was no secret to anybody. Before class started he disappeared to the cafeteria, where he sat among the migrant kids who were served subsidized breakfast. Often the cooks gave him sandwiches to take home. He once told me about a Christmas in which he got a single Hot Wheels car.

Luckily, Chris showed up in time to grab a plate for dinner. My mom felt his cheeks and remarked at how cold they were. "How did you get here, Chris?" she said.

"Walked."

"But Christopher," my mom said, "you live at least nine miles away."

Chris shrugged, removed his coat, then tossed it at our coat rack, which caught it by one arm. He was wearing The Shirt, the one we were all supposed to not laugh at. Seeing Chris wearing The Shirt was like listening to someone talk about their grandmother's terminal bowel disorder; you had to restrain yourself from laughing despite the gravity of it. And so the moment calls for:

The Origin of Chris Peterson's Shirt
By Dick Dills

One afternoon at an assembly, Chris, having successfully cited three safety tips, won a gift certificate for the shirt of his choice from T's Me. T's Me was in the same building as the bike shop across from Arby's, and my preferred place to shop for shirts. I loved how you could pick out the shirt, then select a decal to be steam-pressed onto it. We planned our whole day around riding our bikes together to the store to select the shirt. Chris chose a mustard-colored jersey-style shirt with brown sleeves, then scanned the wall behind the counter for the perfect decal. I lobbied for the one with the picture of the hobo that read "I'm So Broke I Can't Even Pay Attention!" but Chris quickly dismissed the idea. This was the only time he had ever gotten to choose a new item of clothing in his life, and he wasn't about to squander it on a joke. Finally he pointed to a decal over the shoulder of the girl named Candi working the counter.

"You sure?" Candi said, splaying her V.C. Andrews paperback on the counter.

"Positive," Chris said, and the word sounded incredibly adult to me. Then I saw the decal he had chosen. It contained no graphics, only a phrase, written in a disco font reminiscent of the *Three's Company* logo. It read, "So Many Men, So Little Time."

"No, Chris, you can't— " I said, but Candi was already at the steam press station with decal and shirt in hand.

"What's wrong with it?" Chris said, his voice steeped in hurt. What was he thinking? I knew that if I told him the true meaning of the shirt he would feel miserable that he'd wasted his gift certificate, but not telling him would expose him to the cruelties of the high school kids in the bus line.

"I'm just telling you this because I'm your friend, okay? But that decal, it's something only ladies would wear. It means so many men to *hump*, so little time to *hump* them."

"No it doesn't," Chris said, angry. "That's not what it means at all."

"What does it mean then?"

Chris watched nervously as Candi smashed down that handle part thingy on the steamer. I knew he was having second thoughts, but it was too late. The policy here, stated clearly on the sign posted in front of the register, was that once you got your decal adhered to a shirt, you had to pay for it. Candi set the shirt, smelling freshly of moist plastic, before us.

"There you go," Candi laughed. "Just be sure not to wear it in the boys' locker room."

Which was the worst thing a girl with breasts could have said. Now we had incontestable proof that whatever Chris thought the message meant wasn't what it meant at all, that in fact the message *did indeed* have something to do with humping men. Candi stamped the gift certificate, asked if we wanted a bag, and returned to her incest fiction. Once we were outside the store, Chris sat down hard on a parking space barrier and allowed himself to weep.

"One new T-shirt. Just one T-shirt that I don't have to pick out from Goodwill and I go mess it up."

"You can wear it on weekends," I said, trying to be helpful.

"You don't get it! This is spose to be my everyday shirt. My mom said to pick one with long sleeves cause it would be warmer." Chris sobbed.

I put my arm around my buddy. "Who cares what that girl said. I think it's a cool shirt. I won't let anyone give you any guff about it."

"You don't think it's cool. You said it was a lady shirt."

"I take it back. It is cool. It's got cool *Three's Company* writing on it with glitter and stuff. Real fancy. We'll just say it means what you think it means and make like everyone else is stupid. But what did you think it really means?"

Chris breathed out his cry a while. Finally he explained. "It means that there are so many men who could be doing things but so little time to do them."

"I don't get it."

"Like in history class. You know, all these men. All these guys who want to change the world and stuff, and not much time to do it in. Or like all the problems of the world should be solved because there are so many men to solve them, but they have so little time."

Read this way, the shirt made a bit more sense to me, even if the font looked like it should be spelling out the title on a Donna Summer album cover. I held Chris's bike while he put the shirt on and threw the ratty one he'd been wearing into the dumpster.

"So many tacos, so little time!" my dad said, punching Chris lightly on the shoulder. "Grab a plate, Chris. Let us feast!"

I had requested that my mom make tacos for our little party, the dish by which all mothers in our community were judged. Chris's mom made crappy tacos, with store-bought molded shells and meat seasoned with nothing but salt. Raul's mom's tacos were frighteningly authentic, with peas and carrots mixed in with the meat and strange orange hot sauce from Mexico that took your head off with a single drop. My mom had mastered what my household called the "E-Z Kurl" method of manual taco shell frying, resulting in perfectly concave shells that we filled with refried and whole beans, meat seasoned with a special Lawry's packet, Co-Jack cheese, shredded iceberg, and chunky salsa.

"Oh, Raul! What a sweetie for bringing beverages," my mom said. She put the bottles of soda in our fridge decorated with Family Circus cartoons.

"Now I want to make sure you boys are properly fueled up for tonight's special episode," my dad said, grabbing a plate. "Tonight is what we like to call 'All-You-Can-Eat Taco Night.'"

Our dinner table was one where people were always getting up to get things, often things not related to eating. My brother,

Jay, had arranged his Transformers around his plate in a semicircular formation, as if to defend his meal from invaders.

My dad kept score on a napkin beside his plate. At the end of the meal he announced the results. "I've got Chris with four tacos, Raul with five, Jay with three, and Dick with . . . six tacos!"

Once again, a winner.

The only barrier between us and ice cream was a dirty kitchen. Raul and I scraped plates and sprayed them in preparation for the paradox of our dishwasher, a sensitive machine that only cleaned dishes that were visibly devoid of all food matter. Weren't such plates already clean? I had engaged my mother in this debate many times, but was always shut down by the irrational force of her authority. My mom took Chris aside and they disappeared together upstairs. Raul and I knew what was happening but understood that mentioning it out loud would draw attention to something that would embarrass our friend. I heard the washing machine rumble to life upstairs. A minute later Chris returned wearing a pair of corduroys and one of my old sweatshirts.

Jay entered the kitchen conducting a galactic battle with two action figures. When he saw Chris, he laughed and said, "What are you doing wearing Dick's old clothes?"

I quickly collared my brother and dragged him into the utility room. "Just shut up. You don't need to bring attention to it, okay? Just be quiet."

"Let go of me!" Jay said, twisting out of my grip. I had only emboldened him to taunt Chris further. "What's wrong? Why can't you wash your clothes at your own house? Don't you guys have a washing machine? How come you have to wash your clothes at our house?"

"That's enough, Jay," my mom said.

"Is it because you're poor?" Jay said.

"Yeah, it is," Chris said. "What are you going to do about it?"

That seemed to shut my brother up, providing no decent opening for a rebuttal.

"Smooth move, Ex-Lax," I said.

"Yeah, Jay, way to be sensitive to others less fortunate than you," Raul said.

Jay ran crying upstairs to bury his face in a pile of Care Bears. When the kitchen was clean we retired with our bowls of Neapolitan to my room for a round of Dungeons & Dragons. I presided over the campaign as Dungeon Master, with Chris and Raul each responsible for two characters. Raul's parents were wary of D&D, having seen a Tom Hanks made-for-TV movie about a guy who spends so much time playing role-playing games that he stabs somebody, but after many weeks of debate they had caved and now let him play as long as he agreed that he'd stick to clerics as a character type. So he begrudgingly commanded sixth- and third-level clerics named Father Johann and Squire Mike, equipped with weapons no more lethal than cudgels. They spent most of their time healing Chris's characters, a level eight berserker called Bigus Dickus with hit points coming out his ass and The Annihilator, a neutral-evil, half-orc monk. Yeah, try wrapping your head around that one. Together they had been descending the massive subterranean lair I had devised on my dad's engineering graph paper, encountering a mix of Greek gods and monsters from the Lovecraft mythos. The experience for us was all like *Where the Wild Things Are,* except lately it had taken more imaginative effort to get the walls to dissolve, the bedposts to turn to trees. I led my friends through rivers of lava and on the backs of flying gigantic centipedes. Once, I made Raul cry by reducing Father Johann to a single hit point in a pit filled with bubbling acid and acid-resistant snakes. Even through trials like these my friends' trust in me as their Dungeon Master remained.

Today we veered from our campaign into a discussion of the latest R-rated video Chris had watched at his cousins' house, *The World According to Garp.* I kept pressing Chris for more details about how Mork, as Garp, bit the dog's ear and humped that girl in the bushes. Then the dick-biting episode and the transsexual linebacker that Raul refused to believe, but promised to ask his dad about. Humping a dying guy in a hospital, falling off a roof, getting shot on a wrestling mat. Those chicks without tongues! I wanted badly to see it. Slowly I folded bits of the *Garp* plot into our game. In a crystal cavern many miles below the surface of our alternate earth, Squire Mike's penis got bitten off by a succubus. Luckily he had some regeneration potion on him. The Annihilator bit one of the ears of Cerberus, who I threw in there based on a roll on the twelve-sided die.

From the crack of my door we heard sniffly breathing.

"What do you want, Jay?"

"It's not Jay," Jay said.

"Who is it, then?"

"Guess."

I threw a Nerf football at the door, rattling the loose knob. "We're not letting anyone who's mean to poor people in here," I said.

"I'm sorry," Jay said, "I didn't mean it. Now guess who I'm supposed to be."

"A total spazoid," Chris said.

"Jason from *Friday the 13th*," Raul said.

"Quit messing around, Jay," I said, opening the door.

"Look, I'm Chris," Jay said. My brother wore his scruffiest play-outside jeans and had taken one of his too-small undershirts and written on it with an indelible marker, "To many men, so much time."

"Dude, that's not even what it says," I said. "It's *so many* men, *so little* time."

"What's that supposed to mean?" Jay said.

"It means you're interrupting our D&D campaign."

"Hi guys, I'm Chris," Jay said, "I don't have a telephone."

If Chris wasn't laughing so hard I would have kicked the shit out of my little brother. Then we heard my father's monotonous "Exterminate. Exterminate. Exterminate." coming from the stairway. Time to fine-tune our costumes. My mom had laid out all the supplies in her craft room. I was going as Dr. #4 and planned to enter the Dr. #4 look-alike contest. I'd purchased the perfect hat, scarf, trench coat, and wig at Saint Vincent de Paul's months before and had spent the last couple weekends in the shop with my dad, building a replica of Dr. #4's robot dog, K-9, using the guts of a remote control car and some spray painted cardboard. The idea was that I would walk around while my dad controlled K-9 from a distance. This was going to be my competitive advantage in the contest.

Raul planned to go as The Master, Dr. Who's arch-nemesis. The Master sort of looked like an Elizabethan actor. Black tights, a goatee, and one of those ruffled collar things. Mrs. Vasquez had expertly replicated the outfit with her deluxe sewing machine. I kind of thought Raul didn't have the lithe body type to play The Master, but his argument was a good one, that The Master was the most Mexican-looking character in the Dr. Whoniverse, so it was an ethnically appropriate character for him to play. Sitting on the craft table surrounded by notions and bric-a-brac was Chris's cyberman costume, consisting of lots of foil and tubing. As my dad got into a friendly argument with Raul about the number of buttons on the chest unit, I watched Chris survey the craft table uncomfortably.

"Hey, what's wrong?" I said.

"I don't think I'm going to be able to go to Whocon with you guys."

"What?" Raul said. "You *have* to go. We worked all summer for this."

"You guys worked all summer for this. I worked all summer to buy food."

I can point to this conversation as a moment when something about how I interpreted the world changed, like rain hardening in air to snow. I wished I had never invited Chris to watch *Dr.*

Who and that my family would stop being so accommodating to him. This shit suddenly tired me. His parents needed to get their act together and try a little harder to get jobs. It wasn't that I blamed Chris for having no money to blow at Whocon, I'd just grown weary of how this subject dominated every discussion of the event. Because I knew what he was secretly holding out for. He wanted us to offer to pay his way.

"Then don't go," I said.

Chris looked surprised. "Okay, I won't."

"Boys," my dad said, "let's settle down. Everyone's going to go. We'll figure out a way for you to go, too, Chris."

"Thanks, Mr. Dills," Chris said, "but you guys have given me enough already." He left the room, retrieved his clothes from the top of the dryer, changed into them in the bathroom. He said he was leaving.

"Oh Chris, you have to stay. What about the show? It's too cold and dark out now," my mother said.

"No, I really need to get home. I didn't tell my folks where I was going or when I'd be back. They'll be mad."

Which was a lie, but a lie that saddened me. Of course Chris had told his parents where he was going. And of course they wouldn't be mad, whether he came home late or even came home at all.

"At least let me drive you," my mom said, adding, "Are you sure? We'd really love for you to stay."

I knew Chris would stay if I asked him to, but the whole thing was making me feel like crap and the best approach here seemed to be to just fuss over the head unit of my fake robotic dog. I let my mother drive Chris home while we continued to prepare his costume in silence.

"Way to be considerate of those less fortunate than you," Jay said.

During the last official week of bulb season the rain barely let up. We huddled in fungus-smelling semi trailers and when that grew too oppressive got transported to a grade school gymnasium. Raul and Chris stuck together the whole time, butting me away from their *Saturday Night Live* skit imitations and heated analysis of *Buckaroo Banzai*. I hung out with a kid named Clay Jinks who had, in a very real way, fucked one of his babysitters. This wasn't your standard middle school rumor; there'd actually been a locally publicized statutory rape case, and Clay clearly was the unnamed victim. We worshipped him. Years before the drama of the trial I had invited Clay over to play, and he had psychotically hogged my archery set and disobeyed three or four rules of archery, shooting arrows straight into the air, shooting at a bird, running with the bow, among other things. Since then I'd written him off but now found myself sitting with him on a stack of tumbling mats, getting the lowdown on the mechanics of blow jobs. I watched Chris and Raul climbing the rope, playing dodge ball, and fought the urge to cry at the prospect that I might have to go to Whocon with just my dad. In any other circumstance I would have been captivated by Clay's sex stories, but the way he had turned Iron Maiden's "Number of the Beast" into a personal philosophy and his comparison of the scent of vagina to ripe gym clothes made me uncomfortable. So I waited until Raul and Chris were sitting on the bleachers to leverage my status as their Dungeon Master.

"Man, I spent all weekend designing the eighty-third level of that dungeon with my dad's drafting tools," I said, adding, "and with the new copy of *Fiend Folio* I just picked up at Fantasy Land, there sure are going to be some crazy monsters in there."

"D&D?" Chris smirked. "Whatever. We just started a new game of Top Secret. My character is an assassin with an Uzi for an arm."

"What kind of monsters?" Raul said.

I shrugged. "I guess like the Cryonax."

"What's that?" Chris said.

"One of the elemental princes of evil. He's like an abominable snowman with octopus tentacles."

"So are you going to stop being a dick and reinvite Chris to Whocon or what?" Raul said. Both he and Chris looked at me as if I even had the power to prevent them from going. I could see they desperately wanted my invitation but were prepared to act like they didn't care if I told them no.

"I never said Chris couldn't go. I want both you guys to go."

"Okay," Raul said. "Now that that's out of the way, what did Clay tell you about sixty-nining that college girl?"

I faithfully relayed the information to my disbelieving friends as the long-promised McDonald's lunches arrived, which the checkers carried into the gym on palates. Randy, our worst nightmare, barked everyone into an orderly line and forced us to march in place before we received our individual bags of burgers and small fries. The whole production stunk of humiliation, especially with the senior pickers taunting us with their fruit pies. The canned soda was room temperature. They could have at least sprung for Happy Meals.

Then the awaited day arrived, my British science fiction equivalent of Christmas. I woke early and ate my Frosted Mini-Wheats fully costumed. My brother descended the stairs sleepily and upon seeing me shrieked, momentarily mistaking me for some kind of drifter from the truck stop who'd come to raid our breakfast supplies. In the chair beside me I had propped Chris's cyberman costume. Jay patted it on the shoulder and said, "Morning, cyberman," then made some toast, as he had been banned from cereal for a week for pouring himself too-full bowls he couldn't finish.

My dad appeared and I choked on a Mini-Wheat. His hair slicked back, he wore black pants and the tight-fitting, mustard-colored shirt I remembered from the previous Halloween, the one bearing the insignia of the Starship Enterprise.

"No way. You can't go like that," I said.

"What do you mean? It's a science fiction convention."

"Uh, Dad? No. It's a *Dr. Who* convention. You'll get beat up for wearing that."

My father pulled an old TV remote control from his pocket, pushed a couple buttons, and said, "Then I guess we'll just have to set this baby to 'kill,' won't we?"

Then my mom came down, yawning, with her scary morning hair, and we were like the most geeked-out panel of *Family Circus* known to man.

Later, in the car on the way to Raul's house, we listened to the *Dr. Who* theme song tape I'd made by holding my tape recorder up to the TV speaker one night and pressing Record, a welcome respite from the one tape my dad played in the car, *Crystal Gayle: Greatest Hits*. We pulled into the Vasquezes' circular driveway. Mr. Vasquez met us at the door with a gigantic cup of coffee. The thing looked like a bowl with a handle. Mr. Vasquez laughed louder than any adult I knew and got a few good bellowing guffaws from the sight of my dad and me. His laughs never ran together, either; they were like singular explosions of air blowing through his mustache.

"Ho boy! Beam me up, Scotty! Ha! Ha! Ha!"

My dad spoke into his wrist watch. "Doesn't appear to be any intelligent life down here. . . . "

"HA! HA! HA! HA! HA! HA! HA! HA!"

Raul looked like Don Quixote in his The Master costume. As we pretended to engage each other in hand-to-hand combat on the porch, my dad turned down Mr. Vasquez's offer of coffee. We had places to be.

Raul sat in the back seat beside the exoskeletal cyberman that waited to be filled with Chris Peterson. We crossed the river to the part of town that got flooded every ten years or so. Chris's family lived in a trailer at the end of a long dirt road with a column of unmowed grass up the middle that scrubbed the bottom of the car. We parked between a refrigerator and a toilet. There were no lights on in the trailer, but that didn't mean no one was home.

We knocked on the door, three freaks in costumes. Chris's mom, Dorothy, answered in her bathrobe, resembling no cartoon mother I'd ever seen, her face abraded by wrong places at wrong times. She didn't say hello. She shouted over her shoulder, "Christopher. Your people are here."

It wasn't Chris who appeared next but his dad, and I almost fell off the porch. He'd apparently been in some sort of fight, his face bruised, a fissure of hardened blood running from the edge of one nostril to his chin. One of his eyes had swollen shut. On his forehead was a scab the size of a fifty-cent piece. His Peterbilt cap had been sweated through many times, crystallizing in white streaks under the bill.

"What is this fag fest you're taking my kid to?"

My dad, Russ Dills, was an engineer who bragged that he had never hit another person. He wasn't accustomed to the kind of confrontation Mr. Peterson represented. Mostly I feared that he was going to try to subdue the guy with a dead remote control.

"It's a science fiction convention. They show movies and have displays. It's just a fun thing for the day."

Through the space between Mr. Peterson and the doorframe I could see Chris standing by the kitchenette counter, holding a bundle of *Starlog* magazines he hoped to get signed by the surprise guest celebrity.

"How much does it cost?" Mr. Peterson said.

"It's ten bucks at the door," my dad said.

"We don't have the kind of money to be spending it on shit like that."

"It's our treat, really."

"Sorry, Captain Kirk. We pay our own way here."

"Really, Jerry, it's nothing," my dad said.

"I said no, and you can get off my goddamn property."

With the door shut we stood for a moment on the porch, then slowly, quietly returned to the car. I turned off the *Dr. Who* tape at the part when Jay says, "What are you doing, making a tape?" At the end of the driveway where it met the road, my dad put the car in park and turned off the ignition, saying nothing. We sat like that for a good two minutes as he thought, rubbing his eyes behind his glasses. Finally, he said, "This is bullshit," started the car again, and drove in reverse all the way back to the Peterson's trailer. "You boys sit tight."

We watched my father knock on the door of the trailer, then Mrs. Peterson invited him inside. I could only imagine the worst scenarios: a whiskey bottle broken over his head, teeth punched out, kicked in the groin, baseball bat shoved into his gut, throat slit, hand stomped by a steel-toed boot, eye gouged out with a spoon, stabbed in the ribs, nose sliced like Jack Nicholson's in *Chinatown,* acid thrown in face, rapidly punched in nads, arm chopped off with a machete, head shoved through particle board wall, spike through hand, ear severed with an axe, chainsaw to the face, drowned in bathtub. When five minutes passed I considered getting out and rescuing him, but then he emerged, exclaiming over his shoulder, "We'll have him home after dinner!" with Chris smiling beside him.

Neither Chris nor my father would speak of the miraculous hostage negotiation that had occurred in the Petersons' trailer, but later I heard the full story. My dad had demanded that Chris be allowed to attend Whocon and had floated the following proposition to Mr. Peterson. We had at least a couple cords of cedar that needed to be chopped and stacked, and my dad would pay Chris's way to Whocon in advance of services rendered. Forming a united front with Mrs. Peterson, my dad had finally gotten Mr. Peterson to agree to the terms. The side benefit was that now I had to do one less shitty chore.

Whocon was at the community college athletic center. As we parked it struck me that this may have been the first time many attendees to this convention had set foot in such a facility. We registered with the Dalek at the front table, entered the raffle for an as-yet-undisclosed original Dr. Who prop, and found ourselves in a tide of fellow enthusiasts dressed as characters from episodes we could identify by season and number. Soon we realized that there was a freestyle wrestling tournament happening concurrently on the other side of the canvas divider of the field house. While they used a different entrance and restrooms, we could still hear their buzzers and grunts, the squeak of their shoes on the mats above the futuristic music and sound clips playing from too-trebly speakers on the stage. We had come here prompted by months of 30-second spots played in the late hours of Saturdays during this roughly made show that we all identified with. And here we were, all weirdos together in our costumes, boys mostly lumbering along in bodies fattened with microwavable foodstuffs, our faces broken out and our hairstyles afterthoughts. Every accusation that could be leveled at those of our ilk bore fruit in abundance here, each of us bearing the imprint of *nerd* on his psyche with an indelibility that would last through hormonal changes and careers and future success in the tech sector beyond what our Dr. Pepper–addled brains could fathom. We made sexuality-based jokes about the boys grunting next door; we feared their primacy below our surfaces.

"Holy shit, a girl," Chris said, muffled inside his cyberman head.

And yes, it was true, there actually was a girl here. And a cute one at that, dressed as the hottest Dr. #4 sidekick ever, Leela, the Amazonian warrior princess who wore leather bikinis. She even had an authentic-looking dagger. She stood in line to enter the replica of the TARDIS, Dr. Who's vessel, which flashed lights and made wheezing noises just like on the show. She seemed to have realized too late what kind of attention she would bring to herself, the leering of boys incapable of conversing with someone of the opposite sex. I reminded myself of that NOW pamphlet of my mother's that I'd read once, about how women should be able to walk down the street wearing bikinis without being harassed. But it wasn't that this teenage Leela was being actively harassed so much as she caused antimatter swells of testosterone wherever she went, swaths of terrified hormonal paralysis in teenage and preteen boys. We knew she'd walk out of this place with a wrestler.

We watched deleted scenes from episodes we knew and loved. We bought T-shirts and buttons imprinted with the Dr. Who logo. We ate corn dogs and listened to the guest celebrity, Nicholas Courtney, recount amusing anecdotes about his experiences playing Dr. Who's loyal sidekick Brigadier Lethbridge-Stewart. We stood in line for an hour to have Mr. Courtney sign our memorabilia. Then I got third place in the Dr. #4 costume contest, for which I received a ribbon.

"Robbed," Raul said. "None of the other Doctor Whos even had a K-9."

"You boys ready to ditch this planet and get us some pizza?" my dad said, and I know each of us felt a sad resignation that we had pored over every exhibit and gotten our fill of trivia, sapping the convention of its wonders.

After pizza, we dropped Raul off. His mother, Cecilia, demanded that we each take home one of the mini fruit pies she'd made that day. Raul and his mother waved goodbye to us from their porch as we drove away, The Master and His Mother. It was dark, and my dad and I grinned at each other when Chris started snoring in the back seat. The car found its way to the flood plain, where semis carrying cattle feed roared and shook our car, passing us on the arterials. When we made it to Chris's driveway, it looked like something festive was happening at his house, some kind of party, but as we pulled closer it turned out to be three police cars and the sheriff's truck, all flashing their lights.

"You boys stay here," my dad said, parking the car. He approached one of the officers, who led him to Petersons' trailer. They went inside. He was gone for a long time. I saw in the rear view mirror that Chris was awake, and I was surprised he wasn't getting out of the car to see what had happened. My dad appeared in the doorway of the trailer, and held onto the railing as he slowly walked off the porch. When he returned to the front seat he stared at some undefined space beyond the darkness of the windshield. "Oh my God," he said finally, shaking. We knew eventually Chris was going to have to return to the trailer, but we let him sit awhile in the car, insulating him, if for a minute, from his horrors. My father rested his head on the steering wheel and said, "Both of them, my God."

"They finally did it," Chris said quietly. I got out of the car, opened his door, helped him out of his costume, then led him to the trailer. A cop stopped me and let Chris go ahead. Only he was allowed to identify his parents.

Newholly

My wife and I bought the house three years ago in a bout of panic. After our portfolio did a nosedive, we thought we'd never afford a decent place within the Seattle city limits. We're in the Newholly neighborhood on Beacon Hill, an experimental development of subsidized public housing mingling with for-sale homes. Sometimes urban planners from out of town visit to walk around and wonder if such a concept would work in their own cities. Into this neighborhood have come first-generation immigrants from Somalia, Ethiopia, and Vietnam, gay couples priced out of Capitol Hill, African American families. There is a three-year waiting list to get into the subsidized homes, while the for-sale homes linger on the market, prices sliding gradually south. Families who qualify to live here under the guidelines set by the Seattle Housing Authority raise their children in a place that is clean, friendly, and within walking distance of playgrounds, a library, and a community center that provides ESL classes. If you buy a house in Newholly, you're testing your liberal values as if against some formula, weighing fears of economically challenged neighbors with hope for the transcendent nature of community. This place has grown on Sylvia and me, with easy access to downtown, children who beg to pet our dog, halal barbecues in the park. Cultures of origin recede and individuals take their places. There is much gentleness here. I just can't stand it when the Somalian woman next door beats her children.

Seattle has the highest concentration of Somalian immigrants in the United States, and Beacon Hill the highest concentration in Seattle. We're just a mile or so from the Maka Market, a Somalian grocery that was raided by the FBI in the months after 9/11. The accusation went something like this—Maka's wire service, which local Somalis used to send money home to relatives, was allegedly a method to channel funds to the Taliban. During the raid, agents emptied the shelves of toilet paper and bread, diapers, canned food, candy, meat, etc., sending the entire inventory to a landfill. The incident caught the public's rattled attention for a couple days, then disappeared into news archives, though I don't think it has ever strayed far from my neighbors' thoughts.

The boys next door, Mahaad and Musharif, play the same game all afternoon. One of them hides in their backyard storage shed while his brother pounds the door with a toilet plunger handle, shouting something in their native language that sounds like "Oaty-oat! Eye effy eye!" After a while the one hidden in the shed emerges and a great battle ensues, with gun noises and grenades made of dirt clods gathered from the yard's many molehills. They don't seem inclined to play anything else. The girl, about eight, named Luul, appears to narrate the game with a horrible splitting screech that makes it difficult for me to write. I rarely see the father of this family. I've heard he works three jobs, parking cars at a hotel, washing dishes at a seafood restaurant, laundering linen at the VA hospital. The mother, Deka, drives a purple minivan and dries the family's clothes by draping them over the back porch railings. Occasionally one of the boys makes the other cry, and Deka shoots out of the screen door as though she's been spring-loaded into the house, grabs the offending child, and drags him back into the kitchen where she beats him with an implement that makes a nauseating smacking noise. I'm guessing it's a wooden spoon. I reflexively save whatever document I'm working on and stare numbly at the keyboard, debating again whether to call Child Protection Services. I never do.

My wife, who has a regular day job, is never around when the beatings occur, but I occasionally IM her to keep her informed.

> blingmaster2000: it's happening again. i think musharif this time.
> misssmartie: Jesus, call CPS then.
> blingmaster2000: i don't know the number.
> misssmartie: Aren't you on the Internet?

She never provides the response I hope for. I count on Sylvia to bolster my indefensible plea of ignorance and justify my inability to make an adult decision. I escape into my Word doc and interrupt the flow of the book review I'm working on to lay down the givens:

1. The woman next door beats her children.
2. They are refugees from Somalia and are not American citizens.
3. They appear to be Muslim, based on superficial indicators like the mother's clothing and their names.
4. Listening to the woman beat her children offends me.
5. I am resistant to calling Child Protection Services because:
    a. I am lazy.
    b. I don't entirely understand their language or culture.
    c. I am hoping the beatings will just stop on their own.

The phone rings, the dog wants me to extract his chewie from behind the couch, I need a snack. I leave my document open and, when I return an hour later, nudge the screen saver into remission and add a sixth given:

6. I am afraid the government will do something unpleasant to this family if I report them.

One afternoon in late 1998 Sylvia and I were running around the lake, both having recently acquired positions at startups that no longer exist. About a mile into the run Sylvia pointed at a telephone pole.

"What's that up there?" she exhaled.

"Lost-cat poster?"

"Nuh-uh. Revenue opportunity."

By the time we'd finished the run, we had the basic business plan in our heads. Concept: A Web-based lost-pet solution. How it worked: Pet-losers registered, posted pictures, descriptions, and reward amounts for their missing pets. The database was searchable by zip code, breed, fur color, etc. Users could pull up listings of lost pets in their area, then sort the results any way they wished, by reward amount, for instance. The higher the reward amount, the more prominently we'd feature your listing, and the bigger cut we'd get when your pet was found.

We went through a round of financing. We lasted a year, in which I expensed everything I ate. We purchased a television that we never took out of the box, then sold it on eBay at a loss. Sylvia and I always remind ourselves that the one tangible benefit of losing three-quarters of our net worth was bringing Mr. Sloppy into our lives. Mr. Sloppy was an insecure pug we found on one of our frequent late-night neighborhood recons. Never claimed by his owners, he became a permanent fixture of our couch. Slop has always appeared overly concerned about our well-being, spinning in tight, breathy, nervous circles whenever we argue.

blingmaster2000: mr. sloppy misses you.
misssmartie: What's he doing?
blingmaster2000: curled up in his bed giving me the look.
misssmartie: You should take him out on a walk.

I copy and paste the word "walk" into a voice emulation dictionary application, turn up the speakers, and click Play. "WALK," the slightly Latino-sounding female voice says, "WALK. WALK. WALK."

Mr. Sloppy leaps from his bed and places his paws on my leg.

"Hey Mr. Sloppy wanna go for a—"

"WALK."

Mr. Sloppy whines, snorts. Outside he sniffs the beauty bark for evidence of other dogs' urine. He looks like a fire hydrant with legs. A former boss once told me that if she were reincarnated, she'd like to come back as the dog of a childless couple. Slop's got that kind of life. His leash cost a hundred bucks and is made of ostrich leather.

As we walk deeper into the neighborhood, the architecture remains a limited menu of four or five designs. We come to the perimeter, a street of twentieth-century brick houses through which generations of Asian immigrants have filtered. Jet fuel smells menace from the direction of Boeing Field. Mr. Sloppy does his business next to a Stop sign. Judging from his level of fascination, it has been tagged by many dogs. Daniel, a kid I have gotten to know, rides up on his bike, initiating conversation, as is his habit, with questions he already knows the answers to. His Sonics jacket looks ten sizes too big.

"Are you taking your dog out to go to the bathroom?"

"Yep."

"Does he want his privacy?"

"He's done," I say, retrieving the turd with a blue *New York Times* bag.

"How much did your dog cost?"

"Five million dollars," I say, and from a certain point of view, this isn't a lie.

"Nuh-uh. Does he bite?"

"Only little kids."

Daniel looks puzzled. The last time he asked me this question I told him no. "Is this a different dog than you had before?"

"No, same dog. But that's the same question you asked before. You know him. He likes you."

Daniel drops to a crouch and Mr. Sloppy obediently rolls onto his back for a belly rub. "Good girl, good girl, Mr. Sloppy," Daniel says.

"Hey Daniel, do you ever play with Musharif and Mahaad?"

"Ooh, you like getting pet. That's a good girl."

I repeat the question.

"No, I don't like them. You can't trust them. They jacked my friend's shoes one time. They're from Somalia."

"Is that why you don't like them? Because of where they're from?"

Daniel shrugs. "Those guys get on my nerves."

"What about the dad? I haven't seen him in a while."

"He went back to his country."

"When? To visit?"

"Mr. Sloppy likes belly rubs, don't you Mr. Sloppy?"

An ice-cream man arrives, one of the down-market types, an operation consisting of a loudspeaker mounted to the roof of a blue mini van, a couple ice chests in back, stickers plastered to the side door advertising the inventory. I'm resigned that Daniel's attention can't be recaptured. He leans on the door of the vehicle, concentrating on his decision. The driver looks like no one I would ever choose to give my money to, unshaven, smoking a cigarette, ashes falling onto the convex surface of a plaid flannel shirt stained with Popsicle drips. Children stream from their houses, crawl over backyard fences, and approach the vehicle to purchase treats or beg for freebies. Luul, Musharif, and Mahaad emerge from behind a mailbox and stand on the sidewalk. One of the boys kicks the fuzzy border of an untrimmed parking strip. I can tell they have no money but want to be part of the neighborhood spectacle, as if this street doesn't get hit by an ice-cream man literally fifteen times a day. As the other kids thin out and walk away with their treats, I nod at Luul and say, "What would you kids like?"

They quickly check each others' eyes, communicating systems of desire and inhibition. A hypothetical dinner discussion among their family occurs in my head. *Don't take anything—money, treats, whatever—from a white person.*

Mahaad steps forward and points at a sticker depicting a Neapolitan sandwich. As I reach for my wallet, Luul pulls her brother by the arm and scolds him in Somali. Musharif steps forward and asks for a banana fudge bar. Luul, outnumbered, lets go of Mahaad's arm and tries to apprehend her other brother, but it's too late. He's already been handed his treat and runs away backward, taunting. The driver hands the little one his ice-cream sandwich and Luul turns to me, her lower lip trembling angrily.

"It's okay, it's my treat," I say. "Do you want one?"

The driver coughs. "Look, man, I got other neighborhoods."

Luul shakes her head and walks away. I pay the driver and remind Daniel not to litter. He picks up his wrapper and follows my dog and me to our street. Rounding the corner I notice that Musharif and Mahaad have dropped their wrappers in my yard. I pick them up and slowly walk into the alley. I hear Deka yelling inside their house.

"That family sure fights a lot, don't they?" I say.

Daniel is concentrating on a worm that has dried on the sidewalk. "Yeah, one time Mahaad came to school with a black eye. Catch you on the flip side!" Daniel sprints in the direction of the community center.

Mahaad and Musharif are engaged in their game again, banging on the storage shed, yelling, "Oaty-oat! Eye effy eye!" They seem not to notice me. As I get closer, I hear an argument from within the house. Musharif bangs on the door of the shed with a shovel handle. "Oaty-oat!" Bang. The mom yells in Somali, a blurred sequence of syllables. Mr. Sloppy whines. Luul screams, begging, "No mommy no mommy no mommy!" I unlatch the gate. Bang. As I walk across the yard, the boys remain engaged in their play, unaware I'm behind them. When I reach the porch I finally understand what it is they keep taking turns yelling at each other. Bang. The door of the storage shed bursts open. I take the porch steps two at a time. Behind me, a torrent of verbalized ordinance. I beat on the door. This whole time the boys have been saying, *Open up. I'm FBI.*

Deka opens the door. The boys finally notice me and fall silent. Luul stands behind her mother, huffing tears.

"Okay, look. You can't just fucking beat your kids, all right? I'm sick of hearing you abuse your children. I can hear it every time. And I'm telling you to stop. Or else I'm going to have to call CPS and they'll drag you to court and then to immigration and then you'll be on your way back to Somalia. Ever hear of the Patriot Act? That's the America you live in. I respect your religion, your culture, your god, whatever, but I can't allow this kind of abuse to happen next door. You have to stop."

From a distant block the warble of the ice-cream man's truck slowly seeps from the neighborhood. Deka never breaks eye contact. I can feel the boys behind me, hands on their weapons.

"She doesn't speak English," Luul says.

"What?" I say.

Mr. Sloppy whimpers. Deka shakes her head, responds with a long string of Somali punctuated by the words *United States* and *Patriot Act* and *deported*. She looks at her daughter and appears to ask a question. Have I put Luul in the position of telling her mother that I'm going to have them deported?

The shovel handle catches me in the small of the back. I go down in a mess of fists and leash and a bag of shit. I'm on my back. My dog lunges, spraying slobber. I get a broom handle to the face. Another blow clips Mr. Sloppy's front left leg. He yelps, I shout, "You little fuck!" and kick hard, my foot finding Mahaad's chest, knocking him off the porch into the yard. Everything stops.

"I'm sorry I'm sorry I'm sorry," I say, running to the boy, "Come on, breathe breathe breathe."

The boy gulps air and turns it into a long, mournful wail. I pick him up and carry him to the house. Furious, Deka pulls him away from me and tends to him on the couch. Luul crouches sniffing in a corner, softly petting Mr. Sloppy. My left hand is sticky with dog shit. My eyesight is all fucked.

"I'm so sorry," I say feebly. Then Musharif screams and hits me in the back of the head with something hard.

I wake to a car alarm. The strange house is dark, lit by street light through the blinds. I'm on a couch and Mr. Sloppy is asleep between my legs. I don't know if I'll be able to get up. My back and head throb. A plastic bag of water that used to be ice slides off my shoulder as I rise.

"Luul?" I say. "Someone? Hello?"

I find the bathroom and turn on the light. Through my one good eye I see that my head has been bandaged with strips of an undershirt. A bandage has been applied to a cut that I didn't know I had on my right hand. I check my phone and see I have five new messages, no doubt from Sylvia wondering where the hell I am. With Mr. Sloppy under my arm, I return home.

It's a couple weeks later and I have not seen the family or their van. I'm convinced I will never see them again. A truck from

Seattle Housing Authority shows up and a couple guys start hauling stuff from the house—furniture, bedding, toys. When I ask what happened to the family, they shrug. One of them says, "We're just here to clear out their shit." None of the family's neighbors seems to know their whereabouts, either, or if they do, they aren't telling me. I worry about those kids, but what can I do for them now? I walk my dog past their house and am preyed upon by a grotesque thought, a thought I will not even share with my wife, that wherever that woman is beating her children, I at least hope it's in the United States of America.

Acknowledgments

My family: Bob, Nina, David, and Amy Boudinot. Dave Cornelius. PJ Mark, the agent who doesn't quit. My great editor and grammar bitch, Ellen Garrison. Liz Tzetzo, Lissa Warren, Laura Stine, Martha Whitt, and all at the Perseus Group. Wesley Weissberg. Maria Flook, Askoid Melnyczuk, Rick Moody, Amy Hempel. Aimee Bender. Dave Eggers. Eli Horowitz, Aaron Burch, Steven Seighman, Shya Scanlon, Aaron Hicklin, the 826 Valencia *Best American Nonrequired Reading* committee, Stephen Elliott, Trinie Dalton. Roosevelt High Drama Club, Seattle's Book-It Repertory Theater, Orca Books in Olympia, Easton's Books in Mount Vernon. Jane South, Guy Taylor, Brad Parsons, Ben Reese, Matthew Simmons, Suzanne Stockman, David Drury, Sean Carman, John Moe. Christopher Frizzelle, Calvin Liu, Will Doig, Dave Daley, Lee Klein. I love you all.